# "May I come

As she handed him the key, her hand shook and her nerves tingled. Inside her foyer, he flicked on the light and returned her key. For want of something better to say, and because she had never in her life been so nervous, she asked, "Would you like some coffee?"

He shook his head. "No thanks. All I want is you in my arms, and nothing else will satisfy me." He stepped closer, and she gazed up at him. And waited. "I…I don't understand it," he said, "but I need you."

Her left hand reached out to stroke his face, and his arms enveloped her. "Kiss me sweetheart."

Kisha's hands locked around his neck, and she thought she'd lose her sanity while he stared at her lips. "Craig," she whispered, and his lips touched hers—gently at first and then with a powerful, seductive passion that shook her to the core of her being. His tongue searched every crevice of her mouth, plunging deeper in while his hands locked her so close that her nipples beaded. Her body jerked forward, and his right hand caressed her left breast. Heat plowed through her veins and pooled in her loins. She wanted his mouth on her body. Stifling a groan, she forced herself to resist moving her hips up to him. She wanted him then as she'd never wanted any man, but she knew that if she took him, she'd lose him. As he'd said, "Easy come, easy go."

**Books by Gwynne Forster**

Kimani Romance

*Her Secret Life*
*One Night with You*
*Forbidden Temptation*
*Drive Me Wild*
*Private Lives*
*Finding Mr. Right*
*Holiday Kisses*

---

## GWYNNE FORSTER

is a national bestselling author of more than twenty romance novels and novellas, as well as general fiction. She has worked as a journalist, a university professor and as a senior officer for the United Nations. She holds bachelor's and master's degrees in sociology, and a master's degree in economics/demography.

Gwynne sings in her church choir, loves to entertain at dinner parties, is a gourmet cook and an avid gardener. She enjoys jazz, opera, classical music and the blues. She also likes to visit museums and art galleries. She lives in New York with her husband.

Gwynne Forster

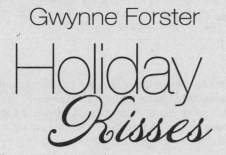

Holiday
Kisses

KIMANI™
ROMANCE

To my deceased parents, who gave me a legacy of faith
in God, instilled in me the virtue of honesty and the
importance of doing my very best at whatever I attempt,
and who shared with me and my siblings their love of
books and writing.

**KIMANI PRESS™**

Recycling programs
for this product may
not exist in your area.

ISBN-13: 978-0-373-86136-1

HOLIDAY KISSES

Copyright © 2009 by Gwendolyn Johnson Acsadi

www.kimanipress.com

**Printed in U.S.A.**

Dear Reader,

This has been a banner year for me. *Holiday Kisses* is my third Kimani Romance in 2009. I hope you've had a chance to read the other two, *Private Lives* and *Finding Mr. Right*.

As with all my books, the inspiration for *Holiday Kisses* came from my own experience. A dear friend of mine is terrified of going to the dentist, especially when needles are involved. So in this novel I imagined what would happen when a romance sparks over a root canal. I hope you enjoy it.

I have good news for all of you who have asked me time and again to continue the Harrington series. Telford, Russ and Drake Harrington soon find out that their extended family is larger than they think. Look for my next Harrington romance in the Arabesque line next September.

I enjoy receiving mail, so please e-mail me at GwynneF@aol.com. If you prefer to mail me a letter, you can reach me at P.O. Box 45, New York, NY 10044; if you would like a reply, please enclose a self-addressed, stamped envelope. For more information, please contact my agent, Pattie Steel-Perkins of Steel-Perkins Literary Agency, at myagentspla@aol.com.

Warmest regards,

Gwynne Forster

# *Chapter 1*

Kisha Moran walked briskly toward her Baltimore dental office, hoping to get some paperwork done before her first scheduled appointment. She wanted to get an early start on what was sure to be a very long day. Lost in her thoughts, she barely noticed the tall, casually dressed man leaning against the doorway of her office until she was close enough to make out his features. She approached him warily, but saw in his eyes and facial expression that he seemed to be in serious pain rather than a physical threat, despite the fact that he easily towered over her five-foot-seven-inch height.

"I'm Doctor Moran," she said. "May I help you?"

"I sure hope you can. I've got a terrible toothache, and this thing kept me up all night."

She unlocked the door, and led him into a waiting room with a large, flat-screen television. She turned on the television. "This should distract you for a minute."

"Doctor, nothing is going to distract me as long as this thing is throbbing."

"Try to relax," she said, taking off her jacket and putting on a white lab coat.

"Look, can't you just give me some pills for the pain? Last night I tried to quell the pain with some bourbon, but this thing is killing me."

She ushered him into one of the patient rooms, where he reclined in the dentist chair. She guessed he must have been at least six foot four from the way he had to contort his frame to fit in the chair. With her mask in place, she moved closer to him and looked down at his face just as he opened his eyes and looked at her.

Until now she hadn't noticed how beautiful the brother was—gorgeous was more like it. His long lashes and dark, deep-set eyes seemed to promise everything a woman could desire. His thin top lip was offset by a full bottom lip that made him look as if he were pouting. She imagined what it would feel like if she'd bent down and run her tongue across his lips. How would it feel to run her fingers through the silky curls that framed his face, which was the color of shelled walnuts? She tried to still the butterflies in her stomach and chided herself for her thoughts, but to no avail.

"I'll give you a Novocain shot, and in five minutes you won't feel a thing," she said, trying to affect an air of nonchalance.

He nearly sprang out of the chair. "Novocain? In a needle? No way. Give me a pill or something."

She resisted staring at his handsome face and let a grin float across hers. "What's your name?"

"Craig Jackson. And I hate needles. Please give me a pill for this pain."

"A pill will take too long, and the dosage I'd have to give you would be too strong. You'd be in no condition to leave the office by yourself and there's no one to take you home afterward. Besides, in the time that we've been talking about this, Mr. Jackson, the Novocain could have numbed your toothache and you wouldn't be feeling a thing. You want the needle, or would you rather take a pill and suffer for another hour?"

"Some choice you're giving me."

"Aw, come now. Don't be such a baby."

"Baby! I'd like to see you deal with a tooth that hurts the way mine does."

"I'm not making fun of you. I know it hurts. Open your mouth please. I really should x-ray this first, but if I took the time to do that you'd be in pain that much longer. Close your eyes and keep your mouth open." She didn't dare let him see the needle. Men were such babies when it came to needles. She injected the Novocain quickly, but winced when he stifled a groan.

"I'm sorry about that," she said, "but that's the worst of it." Waiting for the Novocain to do its job, she took some digital X rays of his teeth and then studied the images.

"Mr. Jackson, would you look at this. How long have you had this cavity?"

"Quite a while. I didn't have time to take care of it. I had to finish an important project. Besides, I dread seeing the dentist."

She told herself not to take it personally, but to think of him as a patient that needed help. Not that she expected it to work. "You need a root canal, Mr. Jackson, and it's going to take a while."

"I don't care how long it takes or how much it costs. I just want to leave here feeling no pain."

"Really?" she said. "I thought that only applied when you were three sheets to the wind."

He'd begun to relax, so she tested the area for numbness. He didn't need to know that if it took longer than usual, she might have to give him another shot. "He raised an eyebrow and said, "Hmm. What do you know about *three sheets to the wind?* I'll bet you don't even drink."

"You're right. I don't, except for the occasional glass of wine at dinner and a cocktail on special occasions. Though I suppose you know that pleasure need not require alcohol. The best highs are enjoyed cold sober."

"I'm not going there," he said, his speech slightly slurred from the effects of the Novocain.

Now, what had she said to bring that on? She could tell by his expression that he'd taken her comment as a double entendre. Well, she wasn't going *there,* either.

With her body pressed against the arm of the chair to steady her hand, she began to drill. But the deeper she went, the worse it got. She stopped and stepped back from him. "I don't see how you tolerated this."

"You still think I was being a baby?" he said, petulantly.

"I wasn't talking about the pain when I said that. And, yes, you were being a baby about the needle. Open your mouth, please."

He opened his mouth, and she resumed drilling. "Ow! Hey!"

"My goodness. I touched a nerve. I'm so sorry. Rest for a minute."

"Are you sure you know what you're doing?" he asked in a disparaging tone.

In light of the pain he'd experienced, she forgave him. "I'm a doctor of dental medicine, a DMD. And I certainly did not imagine all those years and student loans I spent studying dentistry. Open your mouth." She quickly gave him another shot of Novocain and patted his shoulder. "I know it's unpleasant, but at least I'm a dentist who cares that you're in pain."

He looked intently at her for a long minute. "Yeah, I guess you do. Sorry if I've been giving you a hard time." He tried to smile, and she could hear the sudden pounding of her heart.

Around one o'clock in the afternoon, nearly four hours after he'd walked into her office, she removed the towel that covered his chest, gave him a cup of water and asked him to rinse his mouth. He did. "Bite down hard on that side," she said. "It should be fine now." She opened a can of Ensure, poured it into a glass and gave it to him with a straw. It'll be a while before that Novocain wears off, so don't try to eat for at least another hour, but this will hold you."

Craig stood and rubbed his hand gently over his left cheek. He stared down at her. "How much," he asked.

"My receptionist will take care of it. You'll see her on your way out."

He paused. "I can't thank you enough, Doctor. The patients with appointments this morning must be furious with you. Thanks again. His gaze swept across the room and came back to her. Lights danced in his large brown eyes.

"You're the definition of an angel," he said, then winked at her and left.

Kisha sat down in the chair where Craig had just sat. It wasn't just that she was tired. She wasn't quite sure why she was so exhausted.

She knew Regine, her receptionist, would have him fill out the intake form and provide his personal information along with his payment. And for a fleeting moment, Kisha thought about using the information in his patient file to find out more about him.

She'd been around plenty of attractive men. In Key West, where she'd lived before moving to Baltimore, it was not unusual to see good-looking guys wearing the skimpiest of swim briefs. She enjoyed looking at them—after all she wasn't dead. But she had never reacted the way she had toward Craig Jackson. His eyes! She took a deep breath and slowly exhaled. She'd love to experience what those eyes promised.

Three months ago, Kisha Moran had had all of her belongings packed and shipped to number 118 Palely Place in Baltimore, Maryland. She said goodbye to the neverending Florida heat, the floods and the dreaded hurricanes. She loved living in the Keys, especially the casual lifestyle of fishing, swimming and tennis. But after seeing the damage from one too many hurricanes, she'd had enough.

Kisha had been concerned about opening her dental practice and starting all over again in a place where she didn't know anyone. But Baltimore had a large African-American population and a number of institutions of higher learning. She planned to build her new practice by providing low-cost dental care, letting students pay on a sliding scale and offering free service to children from the poorest families.

By mid-September, she'd settled in, had a respectable number of patients. Her practice increased weekly, thanks to the proximity of her office to Morgan State University and its large student population to which she offered a discount. Not all of her patients attended the university, but many of them did, and they proved to be her best source of referrals.

Craig Jackson's acquaintances thought of him as a loner, and to some extent, he was. In his undergraduate days at Howard University, his personality earned him the nickname of *Stonewall*. A brilliant, no-nonsense man, he was often brutally frank and always honest. Small talk annoyed him.

At age thirty-three, Craig's career was about to take off, or so he hoped. He anchored a local five o'clock TV news program and prided himself in writing all of its scripts. His habit of including a "human interest" segment in each of his daily programs made him a favorite with viewers.

Back in his office at TV station WWRM, Craig cast a rueful glance at the chocolate bar, the refuge from desperate hunger, that he kept in his top desk drawer, and shook his head. If he had to choose between hunger pain and the return of that toothache, he'd welcome the pain in his stomach. He answered his phone.

"Jackson speaking."

"Hey, son, how's it going?"

He knew his dad hadn't called to make small talk, so he asked, "What's up, Dad?"

"I'm wondering how far you are from deciding that you want to be a lawyer after all. I just looked at a piece of prime office space that would be perfect for Jackson and Jackson. It's—"

"Dad, I thought we agreed that if I don't become syndicated or get a network-level job within a year, I'll join you. Right now, I'm the only anchor on my level who writes his own news scripts. That ought to tell you something. I've got nine months to go."

"All right. I want you to succeed at whatever you undertake, but this is my dream. I want to see you successful and happy, but, well, I'm between a rock and a hard place."

"I'm beginning to think I'd make a lousy lawyer, Dad. The more I work as a journalist, the more I love it."

"You got your law degree with distinction and passed the bar on the first try."

"But I got my journalism degree at the top of the class. Look, Dad. If I don't have a network-level program in nine months, I'll join you. I'll be as miserable as a wet puppy in freezing temperatures, but I'll keep my word. But you know I have no intention of failing at this."

He told his father goodbye and hung up. He didn't blame his dad. By not joining the family firm he was breaking a tradition that had begun with his great-grandfather. He looked at his watch. She'd said an hour, but he still couldn't feel a thing on that side of his face. Hunger pangs reminded him that he hadn't eaten any solid food since the previous evening.

Thinking about what he could eat that didn't require chewing, he went down and got a container of milk and a muffin from the snack shop. He soaked the muffin in the milk and managed to make it slide down his throat. Then, he busied himself editing the five o'clock news.

That doctor had a tender, caring touch. "I wonder what her first name is," he said aloud, as he got his suit jacket and found the card that the receptionist gave him. "Kisha." He pronounced it several times. She was a looker. And sweet, too. "I can't believe I left that woman and didn't even ask her for a date," he said to himself. "I must be getting old." He realized that the effects of the Novocain had finally worn off entirely when he felt a dull ache. A glance at his watch told him that he had an hour and forty minutes before news time. He closed his computer, locked his desk and headed for the restaurant at the end of the block.

Kisha couldn't get Craig out of her mind and, for the remainder of the day, she thought of various reasons to call him. That night, she slept fitfully with intermittent dreams of Craig Jackson and the way his long-lashed, dreamy eyes teased her. She tossed in bed until her shoulder ached and awakened the next morning, sleepy, groggy and with an aching head. For the first time since she opened her practice, she arrived late to work. Her first patient needed front caps for cosmetic purposes, and after taking X rays and measurements, she got down to the business of making a forty-five-year-old man who should never smile look like Prince Charming. She attached the temporary caps and went to lunch, but not even a good crab salad improved her mood.

When she returned to work, she pulled Craig's file, wrote his phone number in her address book, went into her office and closed the door. Using her private line, she dialed Craig Jackson's phone number.

"Mr. Jackson, This is Kisha Moran. How are you feeling?"

She wondered at his silence. "Uh…thanks for calling. I guess I feel like a guy who just lost the inside of a tooth."

She didn't know what to make of that comment. "I'm not sure I know what that means. Does it hurt? I mean are you having any discomfort? You had very extensive surgery yesterday. I'd like to know how you're getting along."

* * *

Craig's antenna shot up. She didn't call him to ask how his tooth was. A dentist would expect him to call if he had a problem. He suspected that she was exceptional, but her modus operandi couldn't be that different from the ways of other dentists.

"Did you have any discomfort after the Novocain wore off?"

He didn't want to believe that Kisha Moran was just like all the other women who chased him, but he was taking no chances. "My tooth is fine, Doctor Moran. If it bothers me, you'll be the first person to know, and you can trust me on that. Thanks," he added, wanting to terminate the conversation with a measure of civility.

A minute of guilt plagued Craig for having treated Kisha to a brush-off. He resented women who assumed that he was available for their enjoyment, a dressed-up television turkey for their gourmet meal. He didn't want to believe that Kisha was that type. He was as human as the man who worked in overalls, wore a hard hat, dug ditches or drove a bus. He had wants, needs, hopes and dreams just as they did. He worked in front of the TV camera, but when the cameraman put it aside, he turned off the smiles and the charm. His private life was his own, and he didn't mix his personal affairs with his public persona.

Taken aback by what she regarded as a put-down, Kisha busied herself developing fliers to post in the neighborhood and at the university to attract patients. She hoped to have as much of her clientele as possible from the neighborhood in which her office was located. Days passed, and she made no progress in her efforts to forget about Craig. So it stunned her to receive a call from a member of the WWRM Channel 6 TV news staff telling her that she had been chosen citizen of the week and asking if she would come in for an interview.

"Thank you for the honor," she said, "but I can't imagine what I've done to earn it."

"*Citizen Of The Week* is our regular Friday news feature," the man said. "We chose you, because you're offering free care to indigent children one afternoon each week. That's a noble thing to do."

"I never realized that it would be newsworthy. I only want to help the children. Thank you. I'm delighted to accept."

"Great! We'll send a car for you. Please be ready Friday at two-thirty."

Onstage and on camera, Craig looked at the name of his guest and nearly swallowed his tongue. Kisha Moran was his citizen of the week. He read the notes that his staff had prepared for his interview and put them aside. That gibberish would never reveal Kisha Moran's warm and feminine personality. He made a few notes for the interview and, surprisingly, looked forward to seeing her again.

Decked out in a feminine yet tailored red suit with black accessories and her hair around her shoulders, Kisha Moran was stunning. He did a double take as she walked toward him, but he had the presence of mind to stand and take a few steps to meet her as she crossed the small stage. None of the entertainment community's habit of kissing any and everybody for her, he noted. She extended her hand for a cool and very businesslike handshake.

"How do you do, Mr. Jackson. Thank you for this wonderful honor."

Both of his eyebrows shot up. "Thank you for coming, Dr. Moran. Do you treat any child whose parents demonstrate an inability to pay?"

She leaned slightly forward. "Absolutely. I'll only do it once a week, but I'll treat all children under age fourteen that I can fit in on Thursdays between twelve and five-thirty."

"That's remarkable. I don't know of another private citizen who's made such a gesture. Was this among your plans while you studied dentistry?" He held his breath, hoping that he'd given her a question that would enable her to open up and reveal herself to the viewers.

"Not specifically. But I spent a lot of thought on the most effective way that I could give something to the community in which I earn my livelihood. I had wanted to spend one afternoon a week at a senior citizen center, but I couldn't make the necessary connections. I suppose I wanted results too quickly."

"I imagine you'll have more than you can handle on Thursday afternoons."

"Treatment is by appointment. I require that the children get follow-up exams. All patients should have follow-up care. Dental surgery is surgery. Just because a doctor doesn't use a scalpel doesn't mean that aftercare isn't essential," she said, looking him in the eye with a cool and impersonal expression on her face.

After they talked for fourteen of the allotted fifteen minutes, he stood and presented her with the plaque. "Thank you, Mr. Jackson. I'm honored to have been chosen for this award." She extended her hand for a shake. "Goodbye."

"Goodbye, Doctor Moran. Thank you for coming." She had flawless manners, he thought, and he felt as if he'd just had a blast of sleet in the face while trudging against the wind in a winter storm.

He reminded himself that when he sat down again he would still be facing the camera and that he should keep his reactions to himself. But that was easier said than done. Neither by word nor action did she let on that they'd met before. He had expected her to indicate that she was his dentist or at least to say it's nice to see you again. But, oh no. The lady had cloaked herself in a thick layer of professional ice and stuck to the point. She looked as feminine and sexy as he remembered, but that was as far as it went.

He completed the program and went to his office. Sitting at his desk, he reached for a candy bar and unwrapped it. Damn! She'd just showed him that she was as expert as he at giving the brush-off. He wasn't frivolous enough to go after her for the sport of paying her back. Besides, as he'd just discovered, he wasn't immune to her. He saw a lot in her that he liked, but he didn't have time for a relationship. He put his heart and soul into whatever he did, so he'd placed that part of his life on hold while he drove toward his goal. But Kisha Moran was definitely getting his attention.

He picked up his copy of the station's daily journal and glanced through it while he munched on the candy. Suddenly, he sat bolt upright. The six o'clock local news anchor would be moving to a managerial post, and the job was up for grabs. He put aside the candy and typed a note to the station manager, giving his credentials and stating that he believed he was the best person for the post. It was not a network position, but six o'clock anchor beat five o'clock in status and seven was even better than six. Telling himself to put his best effort on the table, he got busy editing material that he had planned to air the following week and when he went on the air that evening, he presented his program on Baltimore's homeless and the rate at which their numbers were swelling.

At the end of the program, viewers' calls jammed the station's telephone lines, and he knew he'd done the right thing. Still, three days passed before he received a call from his superiors.

"Come in, Craig, and have a seat," Milt Sardon, the station's manager said. "I have your application here, and I've given this a lot of thought." Those words sent chills down Craig's back, but he didn't flinch.

"I have to tell you that I never thought you capable of the kind of warm repartee in front of a camera that would make you a good ad-lib mixer with your on-camera colleagues or when conducting interviews. But seeing you sit on the ground beside those homeless people and talk with them as if you were one of them moved me. And your interview with that dental surgeon was an eye-opener. You displayed a lot of warmth and caring, and your viewers could see that. Although you asked her some tough questions, you wanted her to make a good impression.

"We think you deserve to anchor the six o'clock news. Congratulations. I'm expecting great things from you in the years to come."

He resisted letting out a long breath. "Thank you, Milt. I'll do my best."

"That will be good enough," Sardon said. "The office on the sixth floor is much larger and has a better view. I'll have your things moved up there." They shook hands, and Craig walked out into the hallway where, at last, he could let out a long breath of pent-up anxiety.

* * *

Kisha loved the six o'clock news. And seeing Craig in the chair that first night, surprised her, though she didn't think much of it. The regular anchor probably had the night off. However, she took notice when he announced that he intended to change the program's format and devoted a short segment to the questions that viewers wrote or called in about Kisha and the location of her office.

Hearing his voice when she answered her phone at around seven-thirty that evening stunned her. "Hello, Mr. Jackson. This is a surprise, albeit a nice one. Congratulations on your promotion to six o'clock news anchor."

"Thank you, Dr. Moran. You were so formal when we last met that I wasn't sure you'd welcome a call from me."

"Come now. I just watched your program, and I want to thank you for airing the letters, questions and comments about my appearance on your program. You were very generous."

"I…I was filling up my hour with the best material I had. You were a wonderful guest, quite a bit different from the Kisha Moran that I remembered, but that's… I think we'll just leave that until you and I are up to airing it out. Right?"

She laughed. So he got the drift of what she'd said. Good. "If you say so."

"Say…look. What do you say we let bygones be bygones, and you have dinner with me. I want to celebrate my promotion, and I'd like to celebrate it with you."

"I don't know. Socializing could impair the doctor-patient relationship."

"Don't even think it. Good dentists are much easier to find than women who are intelligent, accomplished and beautiful, not to speak of some attributes that I'd as soon not mention. Will you have dinner with me? I'll take you home the minute you say the word." He didn't know why he'd called her. To see her again was an easy answer, but did he want to prove to her that she couldn't ignore him as she'd done at the station, even when she was looking at him? Or was there something else, something that he hadn't defined?

Her answer surprised him. "No chitterlings, brains or rhubarb, please." What a way to say yes. Nothing coy about this woman, he thought, feeling as if he'd had the benefit of a warm fresh breeze.

"How about seven tomorrow evening, Friday, while my promotion is still fresh?" He was pressing his luck, but he didn't want to give her time to think about it. "I'll be at your home at six-fifteen." This time her answer was to give him her home address. If she didn't like the word *yes,* she certainly was adept at avoiding its use.

When she opened her door to him, he wondered how many different Kisha Morans there might be. He'd heard that women wore green when they didn't want to stir a man's libido. But on her, green was as sexy as if she'd worn fire-engine red. He opened the front passenger seat of his silver Mercedes CLS 550 coupe for her and waited until she had fastened her seat belt, walked around and got in the car. "What do you think of Roy's. I don't have reservations, but I know the maître d' will seat us."

"I like Roy's. If this one is anything like Roy's in Naples, Florida and Philadelphia, I'm in for a treat. The crab cakes are to die for."

If he made her happy, she'd have good thoughts about their time together, and he would at least have made amends for brushing her off. "Then that's where we'll go," he said, opened his cell phone and dialed the restaurant. "This is Craig Jackson, I'd like a table for two at seven o'clock, please."

"This is Maynard, Craig. Is your guest a woman?"

"Yes, indeed, brother," he said, knowing that Maynard would get the hint and do his best to get him a table overlooking the water in spite of his having called at the last minute. At the restaurant, he gave his key to the parking attendant, went inside with Kisha and led her to the bar.

"Since I'm driving, I'm having lemonade. What would you like?"

"Tonic water with a slice of lemon over ice, please."

He couldn't help laughing. "Anybody looking at that drink would think you liked gin and tonic or a Tom Collins, right?"

"You get the message. I honestly believe alcohol is overrated."

"Yeah. I think you alluded to that right after you stuck that needle in my gum. Look, I don't want to call you Dr. Moran, although I assure you I respect your title. My name is Craig."

"I'd like you to call me Kisha, if you want to."

*If he wanted to.* Laughing wouldn't make sense, but he could hardly resist it. The waitress brought their drinks, and he focused on her as he sipped the lemonade, seeing more in her than he'd seen before, more that he wanted to see.

"I have a question for you. Is the maître d' a close friend of yours? You have to make a reservation well over a week in advance to get a table here. I'm really impressed that you accomplished this with one phone call."

"I like this place, so I try to stay on the good side of the maître d', and it pays to do that." She evidently didn't know that he enjoyed a kind of celebrity status, and that made him feel special. What a joy it was to go out with a woman who agreed to have dinner with him because she liked him and not because of his reputation.

"I've never been here alone," she said, "so I haven't had that option." She sat forward, devilishness dancing in her eyes.

"You'd only have to walk in here and look unhappy. Maynard would rush to you and get you whatever your heart desired."

"You're joking. I think I'll try it one day. I've never been made to feel queenly. Not that I've minded, but it seems to wear well on the women who get that treatment."

He looked hard at her. The woman was almost as frank as he. A straight talker. He liked that, and he liked her more and more. "The guys you've known must have been a few bricks short of a full load. Where did you study dentistry?"

"New York University. Where did you study and what? Actually, I'm more interested in what than where."

It was a fair enough question, since he obviously knew more of her schooling that she did of his. "Howard University undergraduate, and I majored in Philosophy. Then I got a degree in journalism." If she didn't probe, he wouldn't mention his law degree from Harvard.

"If I knew how to whistle, and if we were in the woods, I'd whistle," she said. "As a philosophy major, I'll bet you were what we used to call, 'loaded.'"

"I can hold my own. What was your undergraduate major?"

"Chemistry. I began my freshman year by majoring in boys, but when I discovered that all the guys were in school to major in girls, I lost interest in the fun. I was orphaned the summer after my sophomore year, and that changed everything."

"I'm sorry. Do you have older siblings?"

"I don't have any siblings, so it was kind of rough. But let's not linger on that."

He looked at his watch. Precisely seven o'clock and a perfect opportunity to change the topic. "It's time to claim our table. If you're still enjoying the drink, leave it there, and we'll get another at the table."

She followed the maître d' to their table and gasped in awe at the sun, a big, round red disc sinking into the Patapsco River. He had seen it from that table before, but somehow, it looked different, more magnificent as he stood beside her. If it was an omen, he wasn't sure that he welcomed it.

Being comfortable with a man of whom she knew nothing about other than where he worked and what he'd told her should have made her question her sanity, but she could read people, and she liked what she saw in this man.

He asked her which chair she would prefer to sit in, something new in her dating experience. "I like to face the door," she said, "but I suppose it would be better for you to sit in that chair so that you can see the waiters approach."

"You're the most thoughtful person I know," he said. "I usually prefer to face the door. Thanks."

The waiter took their orders. Both of them chose the Maryland crab cakes. For a first course, Kisha ordered a sampling of barbecued shrimp, baby back ribs, scallops and buffalo wings.

"Are you going to eat all of those ribs?" he asked her.

"Tell you what, you give me half of your Portuguese pancake, and I'll give you one rib, two shrimp, a scallop and one buffalo wing. It's too much for me anyway."

"Sure you don't mind?" he asked, but he was already dividing their appetizers. "Gosh, this is a real treat," he said. "I get to have both of my favorites. Choosing is always a problem."

"Here's something to commemorate your promotion. Congratulations," she said, watching him closely.

"You brought me a present? Really?" His eyes widened, and his face creased into a smile. "Can I open it?"

"Why not wait till later? I hope you'll like it."

"I know I will. I love presents. Any kind of present. Thanks."

They finished their meal, walked out into the night air, and he held her hand while they waited for the parking attendant to bring his car. He walked with her to the front door of her house, opened the door with her key, entered with her and flicked on the light in the foyer.

"This was wonderful, Kisha. I want to see you again. I want to get to know you." His gaze seemed to bore through her.

*I should say something,* she thought, but nothing came to mind. His elegant style, his charm and good looks were reducing her to a simpleton. She told herself to get it together. "I enjoyed the evening, too, Craig." She opened her bag, got a business card and wrote her home phone and cell phone numbers on the back of it. "I look forward to hearing from you. I work late some nights, so if you don't get me here, call my cell."

He gave her his business card. "I'll call you tomorrow evening. Thanks for a most pleasant evening. Good night."

"Good night, Craig."

She closed the door. "Well I'll be damned. Not even a peck on the cheek," she said aloud. She'd have to think about that. True, she took a chance when she allowed him to come inside, but she wasn't one for making out in public. She had expected a light kiss, since he didn't seem the type to make a nuisance of himself. But a simple good-night and may I see you again? Would miracles never cease!

She sat on the sofa in the darkened living room and kicked off her shoes. Would she have kissed him? Probably. A sensible woman did not get involved with a man who looked like Craig Jackson, a towering Adonis with long-lashed dreamy eyes, a well-toned body and a voice that could lull a woman into a stupor. She rested her head against the back of the sofa and closed her eyes. She had needed that to remind herself of her resolution to never again fall for a man who looked too good to touch.

# Chapter 2

Craig sat in a big beige leather lounge chair in his living room with a bottle of cold beer numbing his fingers. He shook his head from side to side, wondering what he'd been thinking. He didn't have time to get involved in a relationship with Kisha Moran or with any other woman. He knew that if he did, he'd focus on the relationship, giving it everything he had, and if he did that, his career goals would slide down the drain. In his business, a man had to be on his toes every waking minute. He had to keep his eyes open and his wits sharp, or he'd spend the rest of his life as a lawyer. Opportunities were rare. You didn't have any friends at work, because it was every man for himself. He let out a long, sharp whistle. He'd been with her three times, and he'd need a hell of a lot of willpower to prevent himself from trying to see her again.

He looked at the small, elegantly wrapped package that

she had given him in the restaurant along with her softly spoken congratulations.

He opened the package and gazed at its contents. He had several palm-size tape recorders, but when he read the information on the side of the small box, he gasped. None of his old recorders were equipped to download to his desktop computer.

He telephoned her. "Kisha, this is fantastic. Where did you find it. I didn't know anybody had made one of these. This is… I'm speechless." He actually whispered the words.

As if she'd given him a little nothing, she said, "My receptionist's brother works for the company that makes them. They will begin marketing it next month. I ordered it from the company." It wasn't the cost, but her thoughtfulness in finding something unique and especially useful to him that made the gift so special to Craig.

It wasn't Kisha Moran's beauty or that suggestive body of hers that seemed to make his clock tick faster and louder. Physically attractive women were a fixture in his life. What set her apart was the sweet softness of her personality, her intelligence and that way she had of engrossing him in conversation. The woman was like a magnet. He put the bottle to his mouth and downed a swig of beer.

He'd watched her mouth all evening as it moved when she talked and at one moment, he'd imagined kissing it, but when he had the chance, he hadn't. A schoolboy would at least have kissed her cheek, but all he'd done was bid her good-night. He finished the beer, took the empty bottle to the kitchen and disposed of it. Heading up the stairs, he stopped midway and chuckled. For once, his head had ruled his hormones. Still, he wouldn't mind if he could get her off his mind one way or another.

* * *

After a rough, sleepless night, Kisha dragged herself out of bed, remembered that it was Saturday and took her time getting dressed. She liked the autumn. The crisp air, the trees' paintbrush colors and the fresh apples made it her favorite time of the year. She made coffee and went out on her deck to drink it. Looking at her backyard, she remembered the thing she liked least about autumn. She disliked raking and discarding the leaves that drifted down from her tree and those nearby.

"May as well get to it," Noreen King, her next door neighbor said. "There'll be that many more tomorrow."

"I know, but raking leaves was not on my agenda this morning. How're things?"

"I'm firing on all cylinders, friend. I got that job, and I'm gonna be pitch woman for Dainty Diapers. I got a two-year contract. Would you believe that? Poverty go 'way from my door."

"That's wonderful. I'm happy for you. What does the job entail?" Kisha asked her.

"Some public appearances. I was one month from foreclosure. Girl, I've used up all my savings, and I've been eating grits three times a day. The Lord will provide."

"I knew it was rough. Over a year out of work and a mortgage to pay… Well that's over now. Maybe we should celebrate."

"Sounds good to me. I thanked the Lord, and now I'm ready to kick up my heels. How about eating at Red Maple and then checking out the club?"

Kisha frowned and leaned against a post. "I hate going to places like that without a male date. Some guy always hits on you."

"That's not so bad. I met my ex-husband at a place like that one, and we stayed married for seven years, till he reached the age of forty and decided that he'd get all the use possible out of his happy rod while it still worked. Great, if he'd confined his fun to me, but he needed variety. I ditched his butt."

She was not going to touch that one. "Nobody likes to have fun more than I do, Noreen, but I'm not sure about Red Maple. I like to dance."

"Don't be such a homebody."

Kisha had no enthusiasm for Noreen's idea, but she didn't have a better one. "My coffee's gotten cold. I think I'll rake some leaves. Suppose I make a reservation for dinner at seven-thirty. Okay?"

"Works for me."

She went inside, put on a pair of jeans and some sneakers, hooked her portable radio and her cell phone to her belt, got the rake and some black plastic bags from the cellar and began raking leaves. When the voice of Billie Holiday singing "Easy Living" drifted from her radio, her thoughts went to Craig and the impression he'd made on her after being with him only three times.

Even though he was something of a local celebrity, Craig seemed unaffected by his celebrity. On the air, he was sharp and assertive, but with her, he was more…well… lighthearted and personable and didn't use so many four-syllable words. Not that she had anything against them. She prided herself on her vocabulary. She let the garden rake lean against her belly and threw up her hands. How much more time and energy was she going to waste mooning over Craig Jackson, she admonished herself.

She worked until she'd stuffed all the leaves into two

big black plastic bags. "If any more fall," she said aloud as she rubbed her back, "they can fertilize the garden." She'd just sat on the edge of the deck to rest and breathe deeply of the morning air when her cell phone rang.

Thinking that Noreen probably wanted to cancel their date with a bizarre excuse, as she often did, Kisha rested her elbow on her knee, expelled a long breath. "Hi. What happened?"

"This is Craig. Who did you think it was?"

"Noreen. My next-door neighbor. She's a drama queen. How are you, Craig?"

"You sound as if you've been up for hours. It's just a little bit after eight. I'd planned to sleep until noon, but it wasn't to be. I woke up at seven."

"I got up early this morning, too. I just raked and bagged a gardenful of dry leaves."

"If you had promised me a cup of coffee, I would gladly have done that for you."

"Are you telling me you'd come over here on a Saturday morning to rake leaves in my garden?"

"I'd go farther than that to be with you, coffee or no coffee."

Taken aback, she nearly dropped the phone. "Oh!"

"Is that all you have to say? A guy tells you he likes your company, and you show no interest. Lady, I am wounded!"

She laughed, more from nerves than from any humor in his words. "You've put me on the spot. Obviously I wouldn't like to wound you. First time I saw you, you looked like a bird with only one wing. Far from me to bring about a repeat of that scene. Of course, the last time I saw you, your wings were in full strength and—"

He interrupted her. "May I see you tonight? I want to see you."

The urgency with which he spoke it sent ripples of excitement through her. What was it about this man that made her want to stretch herself with him, do things she'd never done, see life through different eyes?

"What did you have in mind?" Surely that cool voice didn't belong to her.

"We could go to dinner and dance later, or dinner and a concert, or we could go down to the harbor and watch boats. I don't care what."

She thought for a minute. The less money he spent on her the better. "Let's see. We could go down to the harbor and watch the boats?"

"Are you serious?" he asked as if he hadn't included that among his suggestions.

"Yes, I love the water."

"In that case, I know a delightful restaurant on the edge of the Patapsco River, and it's not too cool to dine outside at the river's edge. If the moon is shining, it's idyllic."

The more he talked, the more eager she was to see him. "That sounds wonderful, Craig. What time… Oops!"

"What's the matter?"

"I just remembered that I promised Noreen, my neighbor, that we'd go out tonight and celebrate her new job." She pulled air through her front teeth. "Maybe we can do this another time."

"Girl, you still out here?"

"Excuse me a minute, Craig," Kisha said and covered the mouth piece. "What's up, Noreen?"

"Girl, I just remembered a hot blue dress that used to be too small, but with these depression-era meals I've been eating, I've lost a lot of weight, and this baby fits perfectly. Let's dress up tonight."

"All right. I've got someone on the phone." She removed her hand from the mouthpiece. "I like my neighbor a lot, but right now, I'd love to put her out of commission," she said to Craig, her voice colored with laughter.

His deep and musical chuckle gave her a warm, feminine rush. "You don't strike me as being a woman who walks on the edge, Kisha, but there's something about you that leans that way."

"I suspect that's something you and I are unlikely to explore." He was right, if he meant she didn't sit on the side of the road and watch life dance past her.

"Kisha, there's an old proverb that says 'Never declare war, unless you mean to do battle,' so don't force me to demonstrate your recklessness to you. When I play, I play for keeps, and I like to win."

And she believed him. He was determined, and very self-confident. "Craig, although I like games sometimes, I am not inspired to play Gotcha with you. But I would like to know why you think I'm reckless."

"Your comment about Noreen and the joy you'd have in putting her out of commission slipped out. You said you love the water, so I assume you enjoy swimming."

"I enjoy the atmosphere around water, not so much beaches as the vegetation, the natural aspects. And I love to fish. I'm just a so-so swimmer, but the laid-back attitude of the people and the wonderful life close to nature are what I miss about Key West."

"Why did you leave?"

"I got tired of the storms. After my house was damaged during a posthurricane tornado, I decided to leave while I was ahead. I'm reasonably content here."

"Big cities can really stress you out. Wrap yourself tightly in that contentment until I see you."

"Craig, you're like a whirlwind."

"Really? You don't know how wrong you are. I'm sorry I won't be seeing you tonight. Promise me you'll go with me to that restaurant on the banks of the Patapsco. I know you'll love it, and I'd enjoy showing it to you. We have to do it soon, though, because it's getting to be cool for eating outdoors. Will you go with me?"

"That should be a lot of fun. Ask me again. Okay?"

"With great pleasure. You mind if I call you?"

"No. I don't."

"Then, I will. Bye for now."

Craig hung up, and a feeling of pride washed over her. She could have canceled her date with Noreen, but she hadn't, and something told her that it was good for him to hear the word, *no*. He'd brushed her off once, and although she wouldn't give anyone the chance to do it a second time, her refusal to go out with him that evening was not payback. That would have been childish. But refusing to be convenient for a man reputed to be aloof wouldn't hurt her relationship with him. And a relationship with him was high on her agenda. Something about the man moved her.

She didn't know what to make of his unceremonious goodbye. She dialed Noreen's phone number. "Hi. Do you have any coffee over there?"

"Just put on a fresh pot. Come over. I made some buttermilk biscuits, and they're great with jam and margarine. I don't use butter. It clogs up my arteries."

"Be over in five minutes." She washed her hands, put on a pair of loafers, put the figs she bought the day before in a bag and went to Noreen's house, where she found the door unlocked. She liked that house. Although the design duplicated her own town house, Noreen had used pastel paint and large colorful paintings on two of the living room walls and one dining room wall, making the house uniquely hers. Kisha strolled through the hallway to the kitchen.

"We can have it on the deck," Noreen said. "I had dreams of sitting out there in my negligee on Sunday mornings eating fancy breakfasts of imported cheeses, champagne and such with my darling husband. But what he wanted on Sunday mornings didn't have a thing to do with food. Same old routine week in and week out, day in and day out, in bed and out of it. Looking back, I wonder why the hell I didn't get bored with him.

"I was relieved when he finally didn't want to take me to bed the minute he got in the house, but that was because I didn't know he'd just gotten out of bed with some chick and didn't have any energy left. I'm prepared to talk about something else. Thinking of him depresses me."

"You said you're over him. What I can't understand is how two people can think they want to sleep in the same bed, eat at the same table, share children, money, bills, vacation, television, radio and everything else for as long as they live, and then something happens and they get over it. Or nothing happens and one of them falls for somebody else. Thinking about it just reinforces my intention to avoid involvements."

Noreen poured the coffee into mugs, put the mugs along with the figs, biscuits, jam and margarine on a tray and went out on the deck. Kisha followed her with plates, spoons and knives.

"It's not as simple as you put it, Kisha. If you care

enough for a man to marry him and take those vows, and he cares the same for you, it should work. I say *should,* but here's the caveat. Both of you have to be fully, I mean totally committed to your spouse and to the marriage. The hot stuff doesn't last, but love should deepen. If you can't be friends with a man, don't marry him. A lot of women and men follow where that itch leads them, but a smart person will realize that an itch is just an itch and feels the same no matter who scratches it.

"Good sex is essential, but alone, it's not a good basis for marriage. Some men and some women are ready to cut and run at the first sign of a problem. They're not committed to the marriage. When bills make you choose between paying the mortgage and having the drainage system overhauled, or when one of you wants to save for a down payment on a house and the other wants a European vacation or a mink coat, that's when the rubber hits the road. One of you is going to decide to be sensible and see the light or both of you are going to be miserable. Then, when you look at each other, you don't see a lover but an adversary."

Kisha sipped her coffee. She wouldn't have guessed that Noreen King had such depth. "Would you marry again?"

"I'd be more careful, and my feelings about what I want and need in a man have changed, but yes. Given the right conditions, I would. Were you talking with a prospect a few minutes ago?"

"I don't know. I met him recently, and I don't know anything about him except where he works and what he's told me."

"What's his name?" Kisha told her. "Sounds famil… Not that handsome stud who serves up the news at five o'clock on Channel 6."

Kisha cleared her throat, half-afraid of Noreen's reaction to her answer. "I don't know whether he's a stud, but he was the five o'clock anchor for Channel 6. Now, he's on at six o'clock."

"Then that's him. Honey, I'd run from a man who looks like that brother. How could he be single, or if he is still single, is he straight?"

She had wondered the same, but she didn't articulate it then. "I went to dinner with him, and he was the epitome of a gentleman."

"Yeah? Cool as he is, I'm not sure his being a perfect gentleman would've cut any ice with me. That guy's a honey. I hear tell he sponsors a program that gives kids free guitar and piano lessons, and he helped build a playground in South Baltimore right where a hideous trash and garbage dump used to be. He does his civic duty, but…he sure lays it out there on his newscast. Girl, he's big-time."

"Where did you see him? In person, I mean."

"He's been the emcee at a bunch of galas, fund-raisers, awards ceremonies and heaven knows what else. That guy's a big name around here. You say Craig Jackson, and even the kids know who you're talking about. You new in town, but you'll learn."

"Interesting. We'll see." She went home later with plenty to think about. She hadn't learned anything uncomplimentary about Craig, but she wasn't sure that she could keep up with a man who had such a public life. On the other hand, she had decided that she wanted him, and that was that. He'd said she was reckless. Maybe, but in his case, she didn't think she was taking too big a chance. She knew a man when she saw one, and Craig Jackson defined the gender.

That evening, as she sat with Noreen at a table in Red

Maple enjoying the floor show, memories of Craig flashed through her mind while she looked at couples dancing and playing the age-old male-female games.

"Would you like to dance?"

She looked up at the neatly dressed man, extended her hand to him and stood. "You looked about as lonely as I feel," he said. "Otherwise I would never have gotten the nerve to ask you to dance. My name is Josh."

"Mine's Kisha. How are you, Josh?"

"Pretty good. I just moved here from Lake Charles, New York, and somebody told me that nice folks come to the Red Maple. Meeting people in this place is easy, but getting to know them is practically impossible. I won't ask if you have a guy, because that would be silly. Where is he tonight?"

"I'm helping my neighbor celebrate her new job after a year out of work," she said, hoping to steer the conversation away from personal issues.

"I'm glad for her. That's why I'm in Baltimore. My company moved down here, and I had a choice of moving or looking for another job."

The music ended, and he walked with her to her table. "Thanks, Kisha, for a real nice dance."

"Thank you, Josh. I hope you find your niche here."

"I told you you'd get a guy," Noreen said. "The place is full of men."

"Yeah, and one of them finally asked me to dance," Kisha said drily. "How's it going with the guy you've been dancing with?"

"He's pleasant, but the poor guy's looking for a fast one, and that is not my style. Ready to go when you are."

"That was fun, Noreen," Kisha said when they got home. "Good night."

"And thank you for being my friend, Kisha. That's the first time I've been out in a year. It was wonderful. Good night."

Kisha went inside and plodded up the stairs to her bedroom. Being alone was getting to her, but until she met Craig Jackson, she had enjoyed it. She should either go after what she wanted or forget about him and get on with her life. But how did one go after the hottest, most eligible man in town?

When Craig woke the next morning, he was not having misgivings about Kisha, his problem was himself. He had asked her to dinner on an impulse. But he suspected that he'd wanted subconsciously to do that from the day she mended his tooth.

He went to the bathroom, splashed some cold water on his face, donned a robe and headed downstairs for a cup of coffee. "I shouldn't make phone calls before noon," he said to himself with a derisive jab at his own ego. After pouring a little milk into the coffee, he took a few swallows and dumped the remainder into the sink. Leaning against the kitchen table, he happened to look at his hands, turned them over and examined his palms. He'd once played the violin, carved beautiful images and been fairly good at sketching. What had he done with his artistic talents? He'd let all of them fall by the way while he raced to be the next Walter Cronkite.

He'd gotten so used to ignoring his feelings and needs that he failed to appreciate the attractiveness of a woman who had precisely the traits he admired in the opposite sex. And he gave his subconscious a flogging when it led him to do what was reasonable and perhaps in his interest. Instead of being annoyed at himself for having invited

Kisha to the River Restaurant, he decided to look forward to it and see if he enjoyed her company as much as he had during their evening at Roy's. It was time to lead a fuller life, but that didn't mean he'd put anything ahead of his goal to have a network-level job within a year. For him, change would not be a simple matter, and he knew it.

Women of all ages had pursued him ever since his voice changed when he was thirteen years old. Fortunately for him, his father had pounded it into his head that what came easily went just as fast. "Easy come, Craig, easy go," he'd said. He couldn't count the times his father had lectured to him about the travails of a man who, having spent his life trading on a face that was his only virtue, reached the age of wrinkles, thinning hair and sagging jowls and discovered that he had nothing. He had never wished he wasn't handsome, because his face opened doors for him. But he'd worked hard to justify his good fortune, to accomplish something meaningful that would enable him to help others. From childhood, he had wanted to earn respect by stature and deed, and not by the length of his eyelashes, or by the achievements of his father.

Nothing pleased him more than the fact that Kisha seemed to like him for himself. She'd soon learn more about him, and she might not like what she learned, but he'd take that chance. They needed to talk. She agreed to go out with him for the second time, but neither had asked the other that most important question. She hadn't asked him if he was married. And she had the trappings of a single woman, but he also had to be sure.

He rushed to answer the house phone when it rang. "Hi, Mom. How are you, and how's Dad?" He always asked that question.

"We're fine. We're having a rather heated argument

about the *Dred Scott Decision*. He says Roger Taney was chief justice when he wrote the majority opinion that blacks, whether slave or free, were not and never could be citizens of the United States, and that an angry Lincoln retaliated with the Emancipation Proclamation. Is he right? I thought John Marshall was chief justice at the time, but that Taney wrote the majority opinion."

He had to laugh. "Mom, not even a college law professor would argue with Dad about Supreme Court decisions. Remember he's argued cases before the Supreme Court, and he's correct, but I give you credit for guts. Taney succeeded Marshall as chief justice, and he was chief justice when he wrote that opinion."

"You lawyers always gang up on me, but remember more people need doctors than lawyers…or journalists."

He imagined that she shook her finger at him. "Go hug Dad and tell him that he's right as usual."

If he could have the kind of relationship with a woman that his parents had shared for as long as he'd known them, he *shouldn't* ask for anything more, including a network news job. But he knew himself, and he'd never give up his dream.

He didn't question why he thought of Kisha just then as if she were the one, because he knew himself and his responses to women. She *could be* if their relationship developed. Hampered by the worst pain he'd ever experienced, he opened his eyes, imagined looking up at her and felt a charge all the way from his head to his toes.

Kisha didn't question the reason for the casual phone call she received from Craig. It was as if he'd phoned her so that she wouldn't forget about him. But she would be patient, and when he made a move—as he surely would—

she'd be ready. His call had come the previous morning around eight o'clock. When she got to know him better, she was going to ask him what time he usually awakened. She'd bet good money that he woke up around seven o'clock and called her before he got out of bed.

She got up a little later than usual that Sunday morning, too late for church, so she stuck her hand outside the front door, and picked up the Sunday newspaper. She thought of Craig, and his love of fresh coffee floated through her mind while she sat on the kitchen stool waiting for hers to percolate. She wondered why he didn't buy a percolator and learn to use it. After toasting a bagel and spreading margarine and apricot jam on it, she ate what passed for breakfast, drank a cup of coffee and headed back upstairs. Unsettled, and at a loss as to why, she'd decided to go to the museum and read the paper later.

Dressed in dark blue stretch jeans, a red-cashmere turtle-neck sweater, a knee-length gray storm jacket and a pair of Reebok shoes she covered her hair with a red knitted cap and headed for the Baltimore Museum of Art. She frequented the museum as much to study as to enjoy the work of great artists, and she especially enjoyed going there on Sunday afternoons. On her way to the European collection, she glimpsed paintings by Jacob Lawrence, a noted African-American, and turned into that hall. For more than an hour, she let her eyes feast on the works of Lawrence, Joshua Johnson, Horace Pippin, Henry Tanner and other African-American painters.

As she left that hall, she bumped into a hard, moving object and would have fallen backward if a hand hadn't grabbed her and steadied her on her feet.

"Well, I'll be damned. I nearly killed you, Kisha, for goodness' sake. I'm so sorry."

She couldn't say whether it was his weight or the excitement of seeing him unexpectedly that had knocked her out of sorts. "Craig, you must weigh a ton."

"Well, not quite. Two hundred pounds is more like it."

She flexed her arms to be sure she still had both of them. "Two hundred moving pounds is a heck of a lot of power."

He stepped closer to her and grasped her with both hands. "Are you all right?"

"I'll be fine, if I can ever breathe normally again. Don't tell me you like to hang out in museums, too."

"I like museums, but I'm working on a story about the museum's relationship to the community, and I came here to observe the free Family Sundays hands-on workshop. This particular program is unusually creative. I'll be reporting on it in a segment of an upcoming newscast. Are you heading any where special after you leave here?"

Seconds before she opened her mouth to say yes, she was busy, she remembered her resolve to either get things going with him or to forget about him. So she said, "What did you have in mind?"

Craig stuffed his hands into his trouser pockets, looked down at her and grinned. "It's a wonder I recognized you." As discombobulated as Kisha, he stared at her for a minute. "Look. Could we go somewhere for coffee or a drink?" he asked her, more as a gentlemanly gesture—he assured himself—than as a means of appeasing his ever-growing attraction to her. "I…uh…it would be nice if we could spend a little time together."

"It would be nice, but you've got on a business suit and tie, and I'm dressed for the supermarket."

"You look great to me. We don't have to go to the snazziest place in town. What about the Barbecue Pit. It's practically empty on Sunday afternoons."

"I… All right."

He took her hand as they walked down the steps. "It's not too far from here, so we can walk. My car is closer to the restaurant than it is to the museum." He hoped that she wouldn't attach too much significance to such a casual invitation, but the woman was not stupid, and she could figure out a man's motives from his behavior.

"Since I'm here," he said when they had seated themselves, "I may as well have some barbecued ribs. I doubt I'll ever get enough of them."

"Excuse me a minute, please." She left and a few minutes later returned with her knitted cap in her hand and her hair swinging around her shoulders.

"I was wondering if I was going to get used to your little-girl look," he said. "What would you like?"

"You've influenced me. I'll have barbecued ribs, a biscuit and coffee."

"So you like art, Kisha. That says a lot about you. Do you see it as beauty or as a technical achievement?"

"Both." She described what it expressed to her. "It's like the Empire State Building reigning over the skies of mid-Manhattan, or a sleek airplane speeding through the clouds, or Joseph Addai streaking toward the goal line for the Colts."

"You're a football fan? What other sports do you like?"

"Tennis. I'm a tennis freak. I play fairly well, but I can watch it for hours, even on television. It's universal. My favorite recreational things to do are visiting art galleries, traveling overseas, reading and tennis."

He shook his head in wonder. "I'd put travel first, and

if you added water sports, we'd be on the same page. Where have you traveled?"

"Most of Western Europe. One of my fondest memories is being nineteen in Paris and subsisting on bread, cheese and water. When I got back home, I didn't want to see any cheese or bread. I wouldn't have drunk water if I could have lived without it."

"It's amazing, Kisha, how much we have in common. I lived like that in Paris, Rome, Spain and Copenhagen. I slept on the street, in doorways, churches, you name it, and when I got back home, I was ready to do it all over again. Fortunately, common sense prevailed." They talked about their experiences, shared moments of joy and adventure. He realized that they had talked for hours when he noticed that the restaurant was full of patrons. A look at his watch told him that it was a quarter of seven and time for dinner.

"It's dinnertime, Kisha. I'm not hungry, but we can eat dinner if this place suits you."

"I'm not hungry enough for dinner. Let's go somewhere and get a great dessert."

"Girl after my own heart. How about a huge warm peach cobbler topped with two scoops of vanilla ice cream?" Her smile of approval made him feel like a king.

When he took her home almost two hours later, he wanted more than he knew he would get, but his mind told him that, in Kisha's case, less was more. And while he stood in her foyer staring down at her, seeing what he knew he wanted, he made up his mind to get her. But he merely took her hand, kissed the back of it and left her.

# Chapter 3

Kisha did not expect to hear from Craig after he left her that night. She brushed off her annoyance at him for heating her up with his desire-filled eyes and making her ache for a sample of what he promised almost every time he looked at her. So she took her time answering the telephone.

"This is Doctor Moran. How may I help you?"

"Hi. This is Craig. Is it too late to call you?"

She'd have to get used to his voice. It did strange things to her. She sat up in bed and turned on the light. "Hi, Craig. If I don't go out, I try to get in bed by ten-thirty, because I get up early. I just crawled in, but I was not asleep. Are you safely at home?"

"Yes. I'm home. I called because I want to do something that I thought I'd better not try when we were together." She held her breath and waited. "I want to kiss you good-night."

"Oh," she said, after gathering her wits.

His laughter rolled through the wire, exciting and arousing her. How she wished she could see his face when he laughed like that. "Are you saying you're glad I didn't kiss you or that you don't want me to kiss you now? Which is it?" he asked her.

"Neither. And stop trying to push me into a corner. Kiss me and let me go to sleep." She wanted to bite her tongue, but a lot of good that would do.

"Part your lips just a little," he said in a low, whispered tone. "Just enough for me to slip in. Feast a little bit and let me know you enjoy it. Now, take me in fully, and let me love you. Good night, Kisha."

"Hey, don't you dare hang up!"

"Why not. That was the sweetest kiss imaginable, so I thought it was the perfect time for us to say good-night."

"You practically hypnotized me, and I've never heard of anybody doing that over the phone."

"Are you angry with me because I kissed you?"

"I…I don't know."

"Next time, I won't kiss you over the phone. I'll kiss you in person. Will that be all right?"

"That will be fine, and if I'm not happy with it, I'll let you know."

His laughter wrapped around her, warming and comforting her. "Sleep well, baby. I'll phone you tomorrow." He hung up.

And she fell asleep. What would have happened if he had kissed her for real?

He telephoned her the next morning at eight o'clock, minutes after she smelled the coffee beginning to perk. "Hi. If you didn't sleep well, don't tell me. I know you're in a hurry, so I'll only take a minute. I have an invitation to the Admiral's Service on one of the harbor cruise ships. It's really nice. Will you go with me Saturday evening?"

"What should I wear?"

"A dressy dress would be perfect. After the dinner, there's dancing to a live band. What about it?"

The more he talked, the more eager she was to see him. "That sounds wonderful, Craig. What time?"

"I'll be at your place at a quarter of six. Don't forget."

"I'll look forward to it."

"Great. But we'll talk before Saturday. Have a very good day. Bye."

"Till the next time, Craig."


After what seemed like years, Saturday finally arrived. He rang her doorbell at exactly five forty-five. He had the impression that she'd waited for him, for she flung the door open at once with a beaming, expectant expression on her face. Craig knew his face betrayed his delight in her. Throwing aside caution, he wrapped her in his arms. "You make me feel great, Kisha, and not because you're so pretty. It's just…you make me feel good."

Wondering if she was witnessing a change in him, she hugged him in return, stepped back and looked at him. "You make me feel good, too." She'd never known a man who played it so close to the vest. If he had secrets, she didn't want to think about them right then. She wanted to enjoy the evening.

"You look lovely. This is a beautiful dress."

"Thank you. Dusty rose is my favorite color. I like the way you look, too, Craig. Very nice, indeed."

He didn't like compliments about his appearance, but

wanting to please her, he'd dressed in one of his most flat-tering blue suits, a white shirt and a royal blue and dark pink-striped tie with a matching handkerchief in his pocket. He couldn't help feeling special. A man wanted his woman to be proud of him.

Kisha pinched herself. Nothing like being sure that you were wide-awake. She had to stop imagining that she was in a fairy tale when she was with Craig or she'd find herself head over heels in love with him. He'd hugged her in the sweetest and most…well, protective and unthreatening way, and she had ached for a kiss. Fortunately, common sense had not deserted her and she had stepped back.

They boarded the harbor cruiser, and when he gave the maître d' his reservation card, the man led them to the Admiral's Service. She gazed around at the seductive decor with the twinkling chandeliers, upholstered chairs and table centerpieces of candles banked with red, yellow and white roses. Soft music played in the background. On an impulse that she suspected he'd call reckless, she leaned toward him.

"This place is elegant, wonderful. I'd give anything if I could dance with you."

He focused his eyes on her, and she'd swear that they darkened and seemed to gather clouds as he sucked in his breath and breathed deeply. "And I'd give anything to have my arms around you this minute for any reason whatever. I've planned for us to dance after dinner, if you'd like." He seemed to say the latter mostly as an afterthought.

"I'd like it very much." She waited while the waiter took their orders before saying, "All of a sudden, we're moving so fast, Craig, and I'm not sure it's a good thing.

I don't really know that much about you. For instance, are you married?"

"I have never been married, Kisha, and I am not living with any woman, nor have I ever done that. What about you? I decided that you were single, but I want you to tell me."

"You're right. I am single, and I've never been married or lived with anyone. Not that I think that last part is important here, but since you laid it all out, so did I."

"And I told you, because I wanted you to know that I don't have any ties." Their food arrived, he tasted the crown roast of pork that they both ordered and a smile flashed across his face. "As far as I'm concerned, we hit the jackpot. This is good stuff."

"Delicious," she said a minute later. He ordered a pinot grigio wine, and they ate in silence for a while. The waiter poured their wine, and Craig raised his glass to her. "You're a most refreshing companion."

"Thank you. And you're delightful company," she said, sipped her drink and put the glass back on the table. Surreptitiously, she watched him as he ate and drank, always swallowing his food before speaking, using his utensils flawlessly as if it were second nature to him. The summer after graduating from high school, she'd gone to Miss Mabel's School for Girls to learn manners and dress, thanks to a small scholarship, but she suspected he'd learned etiquette and manners at home.

"What do your parents do, Craig? Mine were public school teachers descended from blue-collar workers." Surely that was not a slight frown on his face.

"My dad's a lawyer, and my mother is a pediatrician. They live in Seattle, Washington. What would you like for dessert?"

In other words, he'd finished with the discussion of his parents. She conceded that he had the right not to talk about his parents, though she couldn't imagine why, since she doubted there was anything to hide. Well, if he wanted them to talk, she decided, he would carry the burden of conversation.

"I'd like to have the floating island. I want to know if they make it the way I do with a floating meringue and crème anglaise. It's a delicious dessert."

"I'll have the same," he said and ordered the dessert. "I don't remember another dinner date whose choice of food was identical to mine. It's almost as if we're dining at home or as if the meal was prepared especially for us."

She wanted to ask him where he lived, but instinct told her that it was not the time for any more personal questions. "Yes," she said. "This is very intimate, or maybe it's the ambience."

The waiter served their floating island from a scalloped silver bowl and pitcher. Their dessert dishes were nestled in bowls of cracked ice. "If I didn't know better," she said, "I'd think I was in the White House. I've never considered serving this over ice. I serve it as cold as possible, but... well, this is great."

He sampled the confection and crème, put his spoon down and looked hard at her. "Are you telling me you can make this?"

She ate another spoonful and wondered about the propriety of asking for seconds. "Sure I can and have on a number of occasions."

"May I invite myself to your house? You don't have to cook dinner, just make this dessert. Plenty of this and coffee will do the trick. It's one of my favorites."

"I'll let you know. Probably when I have time to make it. It takes two days, because you have to freeze the *island.*"

"I will definitely encourage you to find the time. Would you like coffee or espresso?"

"Espresso."

"A woman after my own heart." He ordered two large cups of espresso. They finished the meal, and he suggested that they sit in the lounge. "The band begins at nine, and we can dance, if you like."

She got the impression that he took nothing for granted, because he always asked her what she would like and, when it was relevant, he asked how she would like it.

*I could get used to this man in a big way,* she said to herself. "Craig, would you excuse me for a few minutes?"

He stood, held out his hand and helped her to her feet. "Of course. This sofa is pretty low. It must have been designed for children or elves."

She smiled and, without thinking, blew him a kiss as she hurried off to the ladies' room to make certain that none of that pork remained between her teeth. She freshened her lipstick and perfume, checked her dress and was about to leave when a woman rushed into the room.

"Uh, miss, is that Craig Jackson you're with?"

Momentarily speechless, Kisha smiled at the woman as she collected her wits. Before the woman could ask again, Kisha left the room.

Craig met her as she entered the lounge. "The band has started playing. Shall we go?" She nodded, and he slid an arm around her waist. She liked the feel of his large hand on her body and could hardly wait for their first dance.

An usher led them to a table, but he only sat for a minute before standing and opening his arms. She walked into them, unaware that their movements gave an intense feeling of intimacy. At that moment, she wished for a long swirling skirt to fit her romantic mood.

Four or five steps took them to the dance floor, and he held her close to him as the strains of "Midnight Sun" floated from an alto saxophone. The band played it like slow jazz, and every note of it primed her for the man who held her and who danced as if he did nothing else and had always danced with her. Her head told her to sit down or she'd be lost, but her body said stay. As they danced, a new and wanton feeling took hold of her, and she rested her head against his shoulder and moved to his beat.

She could almost feel his reticence slipping away from him as his hold on her became a caress. She welcomed it, swung her body closer to his, and their relationship changed irrevocably.

"Don't think for a minute that this thing is temporary," he whispered. "You are in my blood, and I intend to know what you can mean to me."

She missed a step and then another. "I'm not going to respond to that," she said, but she knew he had his answer when she snuggled closer to him, not to make a statement, but to satisfy her hunger.

They danced piece after piece without leaving the floor and, to her, it was another world, one that included only the two of them. Finally, the orchestra played a seductive slow piece that Craig sang softly. "It's an old Fats Waller song," he explained, "'Two Sleepy People.' It's a favorite of my mother's."

She didn't want him to talk. She wanted him to keep on dancing and singing softly. Lord, if only she could melt into him! The music stopped, and the applause returned her to the real time and place. She glanced over Craig's shoulder and saw the band leaving the stage.

"Aren't they going to play anymore?" she asked.

"I suppose it's their intermission." He walked with her back to their table. "What would you like? I'm going to have a Lime Rickey. By the time the ice melts, the gin will have little impact."

"I almost never drink any hard liquor. Is it very strong?"

He leaned back and studied her. "Have lemonade or wine, if you're not sure. I suggest that if you want to try out a new drink, and you don't drink much, home is the best place to do it. Have whatever pleases you."

More points in his favor, she thought. "I'll have a glass of chardonnay." He ordered a Lime Rickey, a glass of chardonnay and a glass of club soda. When she raised an eyebrow, he grinned.

"By protecting you, Kisha, I'm protecting myself. You are lethal, and if you became the least bit tipsy, I'd have a job dealing with my principles."

"In that case, maybe I ought to down that glass of wine in one swallow."

"What?"

"Not to worry," she said. "I was just dreaming. You said I was reckless, but I'm beginning to understand that I'm not reckless, because I don't follow through. I'm learning that I enjoy *flirting* with danger. That's not good, is it?"

"Remember that proverb 'Never declare war, unless you mean to do battle'? It applies especially in our relationship, Kisha. I keep my promises, and I expect you to do the same."

*In that case, you'd better kiss me when you take me home.* "That's an admirable trait," she said.

A grin formed around his lips and spread over his face. "Did I tell you that you make me feel good?"

She wished he'd stop looking at her as if he wanted to devour her. She knew almost nothing about him, and she was already anxious to let him have his way with her.

"Yes, you told me, and it gave me a warm feeling." She was about to do what she regarded as the ladylike thing and suggest that they leave, when she remembered that they were on the cruise ship and couldn't leave until the boat docked. The band members returned to the stage and began tuning their instruments. If they danced again and he drugged her as he did before, she'd be lost for sure.

"Can we walk out on deck for a little while, or do you think it's too cool?" she asked him, prolonging the delicious feeling of anticipation of being held in his arms again.

"Of course, but bring your wrap." They walked out on the deck, and the cool breeze sent shivers through her, but she welcomed it. He draped her wrap around her shoulders and slid an arm around her waist.

"I need this sometimes, Kisha. I need the quiet and the beauty. I see the moon in this perfect sky, and I want to live forever. Not that I want to be immortal, but I want the moment to last. There's no stress, no problems and no ugliness. It's—"

"And no loneliness," she heard herself say, and wished she hadn't. "It's wonderful, Craig, and I will remember this for a long time."

"It's too cool for what you're wearing," he said. "Let's go inside."

He was probably concerned for her comfort, but it did not escape her that his demeanor changed, and she knew he had exposed more of himself, his real self, than he had intended. Her protective instinct kicked in, and she grasped his hand. Realizing from his expression that he understood her intent, she glanced away from him, but she did not release his hand. He didn't dance again, and she understood why, for she also knew what the effect would be if he had her in his arms again.

The boat docked, and as they walked down the gang-plank, excitement began to race through her.

He parked in front of her house, and as they walked to her door he didn't touch her. He stared down at her, his eyes dark and his face stern. "May I come in, Kisha?"

As she handed him her key, her hand shook and her nerves went on a rampage. Inside her foyer, he flicked on the light and returned her key to her. For want of something better to say, and because she had never in her life been so nervous, she said, "Would you like some coffee?"

He shook his head. "No thanks. I want you in my arms, and nothing else will satisfy me." He stepped closer, and she gazed up at him. And waited. "I…I don't understand it," he said, "but I need you."

Her left hand reached out to stroke his face, and his arms went around her. "Kiss me, sweetheart."

Her hands locked around his neck, and she thought she'd lose her sanity while he stared at her lips. "Craig," she whispered, and his lips touched hers gently and then with a powerful, drugging possession that shook her to the core of her being. He went inside of her, dipping, testing and searching every crevice of her mouth, then plunging deeper into her while his hands locked her so close that her nipples beaded. Her body jerked forward, and his right hand caressed her left breast. Heat plowed through her veins and pooled in her loins. She wanted his mouth on her body.

Stifling a groan, she forced herself to resist moving her hips up to him. She wanted him then as she'd never wanted any man, but she knew that if she took him, she'd lose him.

She mustered what little willpower she had left and pressed lightly against his chest. He released her at once. "I don't want it to go any further," she said at his inquiring expression. His hug reassured her, and she rested her head against his shoulder. "I don't know when I last felt like this…or if I ever did. Isn't this happening too fast?"

"I don't know, Kisha. It's new territory for me. Is there a man who has the right to demand anything of you?"

She stepped back and looked him in the eye. "Neither living nor dead. What about you? Is any woman wearing your ring or expecting you to give her one?"

"No one anywhere. I have dates, Kisha, but I am not seriously involved with anyone. I was once, but that was over three years ago. I got over it."

"I'm sorry if she caused you pain, Craig."

"She did, but I'm over her. I sense that what's happening with us is important. Are you willing for us to find out what it is, to spend time together and learn each other?"

"I'd like that, but it's strange. I feel something for you, but I don't know who you are, and you don't know who I am. So, yes. I'm willing."

He wrapped her in his arms, hugged her to him and grinned. "I'd better get out of here while I'm still batting one hundred. I'll kiss you later." He opened the door and left.

"I knew I'd never be the same," she said to herself, "and one kiss was all it took."

# Chapter 4

*N*ow *what!*

The walls around her had not changed color, and the stairs remained as they were when she left home earlier that morning. Something…no, everything had changed. She floated up the stairs to her bedroom, certain that if she didn't manage somehow to anchor herself, she'd fly. She fell backward on her bed, flung out her arms and then hugged herself.

"One of these days, I'm going to know who that man is deep down inside of him where he lives, and I'm never going to let him go. Never," she sang out. Then she jumped up, hugged herself again and skipped to the bathroom. She had barely finished her ablutions and crawled into bed when the telephone rang. She didn't look at the caller ID.

"Hi. Are you home already?"

"I just walked in. I wanted to say good-night, and I

didn't want to risk calling you too late. Kisha, I'm still awed by what happened between us an hour ago. It seems unreal. Yet, I know it happened and that it's the real thing, at least for me. What about you?"

"Craig, I'm still in the clouds. If you ask me again tomorrow afternoon or evening, I might give you an intelligent answer." She couldn't help laughing at that. The man had knocked her for a loop.

"At least you feel it, too." She heard the satisfaction that his voice conveyed. "Does it surprise you that I want to see you tomorrow?"

"I don't know. It's… I don't know."

"Then I'll phrase it this way, Kisha. Would you like us to be together tomorrow?"

The man didn't pull his punches, and she could do no less. "What will we do?" she asked him, unaware that, to his mind, she always found a way to avoid using the word, yes.

"I'm thinking about a future special report, and you could help me with my research. I was planning a story on the extent to which people are resorting to rent parties as they did during the Great Depression. If a person went to your rent party, you were expected to return the favor. The host served simple food—stewed collards, pigs' feet, spareribs, potato salad, fried catfish—and guests played cards, danced and knocked back a drink or two. I'm going to check to see if anyone's doing anything like that now. If so, I'll do a story."

"You wouldn't expose anyone, would you?"

"Of course not. Far be it from me to aggravate a poor guy's problems."

"If that doesn't work out, what about a movie?"

"That's a great idea. Do you want to see the new Will Smith movie?"

The eagerness in his voice excited her, and she rolled over on her belly, hugging the pillow and savoring the passion that enveloped her. "What a lovely idea," she said, thinking that she had never been kissed in a movie theater, and wondering if he'd be that bold.

"Okay. Suppose I come for you at about two o'clock."

"I'm looking forward to seeing you."

Craig hung up and looked around the darkened room. He was exhilarated, and yet he was also feeling something else. A subtler, indefinable feeling, one with which he'd had no prior familiarity. And it bothered him. On one hand, he wasn't ready to be involved seriously in a relationship but, on the other hand, his need for Kisha seemed to increase by the hour. And he had neither the desire nor the will to turn away from a woman who made him feel as Kisha did.

In his arms she melted into him, giving herself without inhibitions, meeting his demands. He wondered what she'd be like as a lover, and the thought of her writhing beneath him sent frissons of heat shooting through his veins and settling in his groin. She'd think him crazy if he phoned her again that night, but he yearned to talk with her again. He flicked on the light in hopes of altering his mood.

Sitting in one of his favorite big brown leather chairs, he directed his gaze to the cathedral ceiling. He knew the co-op apartment was too big for a bachelor, but it was precisely what he wanted. He had never experienced a desire for company...until now.

He jumped up and stretched out his arms as if pushing back the admission that he might not be able to exclude Kisha Moran from his life, or that if he did, she'd leave a deep, gaping hole. He suspected that his reservations about a relationship with her meant nothing. If he didn't have to focus on his work… He didn't bother to finish that thought, because he not only had to focus on it, he had to succeed. He did not want to practice law, but if he didn't have a network job by March 15, he'd have to keep his promise to his dad and join his father's firm.

Kisha didn't believe that anything about life was preordained. On more than one occasion, she had changed the course of events. And she'd done that with perseverance, hard work and intelligent attention to her world and its opportunities. Craig Jackson liked her a lot, sometimes against his will, she thought. But if he wanted to avoid a deep and lasting relationship, he'd get no help from her.

She opened her door to Craig that Sunday afternoon with her hair in a ponytail, wearing the tightest stretch jeans she had, a red scoop neck sweater and a pair of sneakers. She ignored his puzzled expression. To her mind, a man should be kept guessing. Besides, she didn't always dress like a businesswoman and even less often like a siren.

"Hi. Come in," she said with a hushed breathlessness that caused him to raise both eyebrows. And it wasn't pretend. The excitement of seeing him had momentarily disconcerted her.

"Thanks. For a minute there, I thought you were your sister."

"I don't have a sister." She reached up to kiss him on his cheek, and he locked her to his body so fiercely that she thought he might be annoyed with her.

"Kiss me. Put your arms around me and kiss me," he said in a voice that had a compelling ring of urgency and command. She didn't take offense, because kissing him was exactly what she wanted to do. But she didn't get the passion from him that she expected. His gentle kiss was a demand for sweetness and deep caring. When she parted her lips, he eased into her gently, stroking her back, loving and cherishing her. She looked at him with what she supposed was a question in her eyes. His smile and hug told her that they shared a similar feeling.

His planned itinerary surprised her. She was unfamiliar with most Baltimore neighborhoods other than her own, and he'd taken her to the poorest area she'd seen since moving to Baltimore. In response to her question about his interest in the theaters located in poor neighborhoods, he replied, "They're symptomatic of what's happening in urban America."

She knew he was right. "What do you want to happen as a result of your report?"

"I'd like to see the area revitalized. I want to see poor people get a fair shake."

That comment told her more about him than anything else he'd said or done. He was cool and polished, but he had deep feelings for those less fortunate than he.

"It would be great if someone could put together a consortium to rebuild this neighborhood and make it a beautiful oasis for low-income people," she said.

"Interesting idea, but even people with a healthy streak of altruism will demand some profit. Mind if I put that idea out at the end of my report?"

"If you think it's worthwhile, by all means, do it."

He reached for his camera. "I need some pictures, but before this is aired, I'm coming down here with a cameraman."

* * *

When she got out of the car, she had to step over broken glass and decaying refuse. "How do the people who live here tolerate this?" she asked aloud to no one in particular.

"I shouldn't have brought you here," he said, "But I confess I didn't know it was this bad. Let's go."

"I can take it, Craig. After all, I can leave here and go to my pristine neighborhood. These people can't."

He stared at her for a minute. Suddenly he smiled, shaking his head as he did so. "I owe you a kiss for that." Still, she noticed that he didn't linger there. "I'll finish this another time," he said, opened the passenger door and helped her into the seat. He drove back to clean, quiet Charles Street and parked in a public parking garage. The brisk wind sent a whiff of cold air through her and, as they walked, she snuggled closer to him.

"The theater's right around the corner," he said, "but we can stop in there for a few minutes, if you'd like." He nodded toward a coffee shop.

"Thanks, but I'm okay. It'll probably take me a while to get used to cold weather."

In the theater, he bought two larges bags of buttered popcorn and gave one to her. They sat near the aisle, holding hands and eating popcorn, each deep in thought and barely aware of the movie. Near the end of the movie, he slouched down in his seat and put his left arm around her. She looked over at him, wondering about his mood. For ninety minutes he'd loosely held her hand, but he hadn't said one word to her, and now this. He had a strange way of letting her know that he cared for her.

As they left the theater, he continued to hold her hand, but didn't speak while they walked to the garage. When they reached his car, he opened the door for her, but instead of helping her to get in, he leaned against the door and looked down at her.

"I feel terrible about taking you through that neighborhood. If I'd known—"

She shushed him with the gentle touch of the back of her hand. "I'm not sorry I was there. I've decided that that's the area where I should advertise free dental care."

"Give me the signs, and I'll take them down there. I'd rather you didn't go down there alone."

She hadn't seen him in this frame of mind. She was about to tell him thanks, but she'd do it, when it occurred to her that he needed to do it. "Thank you," she said, "but I don't want it to be a burden for you."

"Nothing that I do for you could possibly be a burden, Kisha." He took a deep breath. "Something good is happening between us. It's… I'm not sure I can define it, and I confess I haven't welcomed it. But when I'm with you I feel great, and when I'm not with you, I can hardly wait until I'm with you again."

Suddenly, he sucked in his breath, wrapped her in his strong arms and stared down at her with fiery, eyes. "Kiss me. Love me. I need you, Kisha." His lips brushed hers, tentatively as if he'd never kissed her. And then, as if his reserve abandoned him, his lips and tongue pressed for entrance, and she could feel the tremors that shook him as he gave himself to her. With his masculinity captivating and surrounding her, he possessed her. Stunned, she opened up to him, receiving his passion, the loving he gave her, and poured out her feelings to him.

The headlights of an approaching car brought them back to reality. He hugged her, opened the door wider and when she sat down, he closed the car door. The fire still raged in her, but she did what she could to contain it. She sensed that it was not the time to make demands, but to accept what he offered. And he had just offered her more than she'd thought he possessed.

"If you have those fliers ready, I'll stop by your office for them at about ten in the morning. I'll distribute them in the right neighborhoods."

Emotionally, he'd touched her deeply, but her head flirted with annoyance. "Craig, you just kissed me until I felt as if I were about to evaporate, but after that life-changing kiss, your first words to me are about some…some fliers. I want you to hold me and tell me you meant it."

He pulled her into his arms. "Whatever you got from me a minute ago was uncalculated. It was what I felt and what I needed. I'm trying not to promise more than I can give, sweetheart. I told you this is new territory for me. I'm finding my way as I go along. Don't be afraid, Kisha. I am not going to hurt you." He spread kisses over her face. Sweet, feathery kisses.

"But you told me that there was once someone special in your life."

"And so there was. But this is different. Very different."

She could not have imagined the difference. She was a tender, caring woman, kind and giving, who didn't need constant assurance of her importance. She knew who she was, and she was satisfied with that. He'd never known a woman like her, including the one he'd thought he loved, and who he'd asked to marry him. He wasn't ready to declare himself. He didn't know if he'd reached that point or ever would, but no sooner had he left her than the yearning to see her again began eating at him.

A few nights later as he maneuvered his car through the windy, rain-drenched city, he remembered that she usually walked to and from work and decided to meet her at her office and take her home. The traffic stalled, and he turned off Echodale and headed south to Shirley Avenue, battling the snarled traffic. At five minutes to nine—she gave the children free dental care on Thursdays from one to nine— he drove up to the building that housed her office, parked and was about to get out of the car when his heart seemed to stop beating. Kisha Moran walked out of the building laughing and talking with another man. He sat there, hardly able to breathe. Déjà vu. She turned the corner with the man, who seemed to be about his age, and disappeared from sight. After nearly an hour, he turned the ignition and headed home.

Although he knew he saw Kisha, enjoying another man's company, he didn't want to believe it. Almost four years had passed since the night he declared himself a fool. He'd sworn it wouldn't happen again, but Kisha Moran had blindsided him when he was vulnerable. He parked, went inside his apartment and sat down in his darkened living room, picked up the remote control and flicked on the lights.

Leaning back against the sofa, he shook his head. He'd done the same thing the night he returned from a six-month assignment in Paris, walked into his fiancée's apartment and found her in bed with another man. They'd been in such a hurry that they had neglected to lock the door. He'd knocked the man off her and, without a word, walked out. He forced her to return the diamond he'd given her and

took it back to the store where he bought it. He sat there
for half an hour, went to the bar, poured three fingers of
vodka down his throat and went to bed.

The next day, he had finished distributing her fliers in a
poor neighborhood, had done the necessary research for his
report on neglected communities—he had decided to
broaden the story—and had tried to go about life as usual.
After the story aired, the *Sun Times* and the *Afro-American*
applauded his efforts, and he got a solid pat on the back from
his boss, but the rewards seemed hollow. The accolades
would have been so much sweeter if he could have shared
his success with Kisha. But he couldn't, and he knew he
wouldn't hear from her, because he hadn't telephoned her
or seen her since that rainy night three weeks earlier. It surprised him that her betrayal could hurt him so badly.

"Oh, what the hell," he said aloud. "I'm not going to
waste any more of my life worrying about this." He reached
across his desk, picked up the recorder and began to dictate
his lead story for the evening news.

Kisha became depressed after not hearing from Craig.
She had wondered why he stopped phoning her, but since
his last words to her were that he'd call her, she told herself
that, if they ever talked again, he would have to initiate the
conversation. Still, a nagging pain remained in her heart,
and she decided that she'd just have to live with it. But it
definitely would not kill her.

Three weeks after she began her Thursday afternoon
and evening "children's hours," a reporter from the *Evening
Post* visited her. "How long are you planning to continue
this service?" he asked her.

"Until I'm too old or too sick and as long as there are children in this city whose parents can't afford to pay, I guess."

She realized that her answer hadn't satisfied him when the man asked, "Have you had special training in pediatric dentistry?"

"My credentials are perfect for what I do. I'm qualified to care for dental patients of any age and with any problem, including surgical problems," she replied after a moment of hesitation. "Now, if you'll excuse me, I have work to do," she said, bristling and not bothering to hide it. "If you're looking for a hot story that will enhance your career, you've just wasted both my time and yours."

Still angry, she went to her workroom and looked at the little girl sitting in the chair. "Nadine, darling, you were just here two days ago. You shouldn't have a problem. Where does it hurt?"

The child handed her a lollipop and smiled. "I don't hurt anywhere, Dr. Moran. I just like to be here, because you're so nice to me. I told my foster mother my tooth hurt so I could bring you this lollipop."

Kisha leaned over and hugged the little girl. It didn't compensate for the absence of Craig's warmth, but it made her feel loved. "Thank you for my lollipop, Nadine. I appreciate it, but I want you to promise me that you will always tell the truth. You told your foster mother a fib."

"I know, but I'm usually good," the child said and smiled as if she hadn't been reprimanded.

She kissed Nadine's forehead and went to her next patient. Craig's withdrawal from her left a void in her life, but the children that she cared for gave her love that, while not bridging the gap, helped her accommodate to it. She hadn't spent a great deal of time with small children, and she was discovering that she enjoyed them. She'd begun to experience a more pressing desire for some of her own.

Saturday arrived, and Kisha couldn't decide what to do with herself. "You ought to get busy with your painting," Noreen said. "If I had your talent, I'd put it to better use than you're doing. By the way what ever happened to Mr. Wonderful? You haven't mentioned him since I don't know when. That was a short fling, but it was too intense for me to believe you just dropped him for no reason. Not that gorgeous brother."

"If you don't mind, Noreen, I'd rather not discuss him."

"Did you see that powerful report he gave on slum communities in Baltimore?"

Kisha released a long breath. "Yes. I saw it. It was the best he's done."

Noreen looked toward the blue ceiling in her kitchen, bit her bottom lip and said, "And that didn't give you an excuse to make up with him?"

"Quit fishing, Noreen. When Craig Jackson and I get back together—if we do—he'll be the one to initiate it. Subject closed." She went home, put on some warmer clothing, got into her car and drove off. She'd stop when she saw something that interested her.

If Kisha was in a state of bewilderment, that was the least that could be said of Craig's predicament. He awakened around three o'clock that morning and sat bolt upright. Perspiration dampened his upper body, and his heart pounded wildly. He drew his knees up, rested his folded arms on them and lowered his chin to his arms. He couldn't stand it. For what seemed like hours, he'd chased Kisha up a steep hill, and though she'd always been within his grasp, he hadn't been able to catch her. He'd had that nightmare for two consecutive nights, and no one had to explain its significance to him.

Certain that he wouldn't go back to sleep, he went to the kitchen and got a cup of instant coffee. He was damned if he'd capitulate and call her. He showered, dressed, worked at home until seven and left for the studio. Now what? He tossed the day's journal into the trash and dialed his boss's phone number. Relieved when he got an answer, in view of the hour, he told himself to cool off.

"This is Craig. I just read today's journal. It says you've assigned Roy Gaines to report on that mysterious fire in the area I just covered. Is that a mistake, or does he know those people better than I do?"

"Well, no. I just thought you might want to focus on some other areas."

"Areas more interesting to my viewers than this one? I'd like to know exactly where that could be." He wasn't in the habit of calling his boss on the carpet, but right then, he wanted all that he was entitled to, and if he didn't get it, he'd put his briefcase in some other desk.

"What's eating you, Craig? I don't recall your delight in investigating and reporting on fires, but if you want the job..."

No point in shooting himself in the foot because of his hurt and anger at Kisha. "I'm not asking you to change the assignment, Milt. I simply wanted to know what's going on. Less than a month ago, I turned in what you said was a laudable job on that area."

"I see your point, Craig. You'll get yours. Roy needs that experience, and you don't. The states are getting ready to build a new highway cutting through Western Maryland

and Pennsylvania and through a lot of private property. Know anything about a property owner's lawful rights in that context?

"You bet I do." Craig's fingers began to itch for the pleasure of delving into the project. "When do I start?"

"I'll send you a memo sometime today outlining your budget. I'd like an estimate within the next three weeks as to when you can air it."

"Great. I'll get right on it."

He hung up, rubbed his hands together as if anticipating a feast, reached for the phone to call Kisha, hung up and slumped in his chair. "She's everywhere all the time. Why the hell can't I get her out of my system?" he said aloud and slammed his fist on his desk.

He awakened the following morning around two o'clock tortured by the same nightmare, his body damp with perspiration and his heart thumping wildly. In his nightmare, he chased her again, but she reached the mountaintop, scaled it and disappeared on the other side. When he reached for her, he awoke as he began to tumble backward.

Later than morning, tired and haggard from sleeplessness and nightmares, he got into the TV station's Ford Crown Victoria and headed for Cumberland in the westernmost part of Maryland.

"Good afternoon, sir," he said to a man who opened the door of a house that sat in the path of the proposed highway, explained his mission and asked for an interview. He sat in the living room of the small frame house, and after getting permission, recorded the conversation. Long after leaving the man, who was panic-stricken at the prospect of losing his home, Craig sat in this home office reading the conversation on his computer screen. His thoughts went back to when she gave him the recorder, wrapped in gold paper with a green silk ribbon. He opened his desk drawer took out the paper and the ribbon put it back, closed the drawer and dialed her cell phone number.

Kisha looked at the caller ID pane on her cell phone, saw a blank and wrestled with the temptation to ignore it. But the ringing persisted, and she pushed the button. "Hello. This is Dr. Moran. How may I help you?"

"Hello, Kisha, this is Craig. I need to see you."

"What on earth for? Something wrong with your tooth? If you thought I murdered someone, you should at least have called and asked me if I was guilty."

"You've passed judgment, and I deserve it, but would you please give me an hour of your time. Name the place."

"Okay, let's meet for coffee tomorrow at The Pastry Nook a block south of my office."

"What time?"

"Five-thirty."

"I'll be there, and I'll look forward to it. Will you?"

"I certainly would like to know why I haven't heard from you in almost three weeks."

"Goodbye for now, Kisha."

Kisha waited impatiently for her meeting with Craig. Dressed conservatively in a blue, woolen dress and camel hair coat, she arrived at The Pastry Nook at five thirty-five and, as she expected, he was waiting at a bistro table in the rear of the little shop. He rose and met her halfway, and from his demeanor, she concluded that he was more than a little troubled.

"Hello, Kisha. Thanks for agreeing to meet me."

"Hello, Craig. I thought maybe you'd look different, somehow. But you still look the same."

"No, I haven't changed, but I want to know if you have." He called the waitress, and they each ordered cappuccino. "Kisha, I know I should have talked to you about the night it happened. But my imagination got the better of me. It's tearing me apart, and I have to know for sure."

She leaned back in the chair and gazed at Craig. "What are you talking about?"

"I was driving home one Thursday night in a windy rainstorm, and remembered that you don't drive to work and that you worked late that night. So I decided to stop by your office and drive you home. As I parked in front of the building, you walked out of it with a man with whom you obviously enjoyed a close relationship. The two of you were laughing and walking and seemed to be fairly intimate. I assumed that you were dating him, and I was deeply hurt."

"And you decided that I was a cheat."

"I didn't say that, but I admit that seeing you with him took the wind out of me, and I'd like to know if that man or any other man means something to you."

"You once asked me if there was another man in my life, and I said no. Do you think I lied? Why didn't you ask me about the man you saw me with that night? Oh. I know. Your pride wouldn't let you. I'm disappointed, Craig. For three weeks you ignored me, and now you want me to answer a question that you should have asked me weeks ago. Is that man something to me? Yes, he is."

If there was such a thing as seeing pain, she saw it in the expression on Craig Jackson's face. For three long weeks his silence had hurt her, but she could not bear to cause him pain. "All right," she said, her voice softened by her sympathy for him. "He is a colleague. He takes my patients when I'm not available, and I substitute for him when necessary. We've been buddies since our college days, and we were classmates in dental school. He's married, and I'm his daughter's godmother."

He shook his head in dismay. "I'll have a hard time making up for a mistake that I learned long ago to avoid. I don't see how you can forgive me." He held the coffee cup to his lips, but quickly put it down. "Don't think I haven't suffered for it. I have. Every night, I have nightmares in which you torture me." He leaned forward. "Kisha, is there any way that you can forgive me?"

She needed to understand why it happened, because she didn't want to get involved with a man who couldn't trust her. "Why did you make such a hasty judgment, Craig?"

"It isn't an excuse, but here's why. Four years ago I returned from a six-month assignment in Paris, walked into my fiancée's house and found her in bed with a man. From that time on, I've had only the most shallow relationships. I resisted becoming attached to you, but you were different. Everything about you appeals to me, and…and I need what you offer." A half laugh slipped out of him. "And I don't mean as a dentist, but as a woman."

"How can I be sure you won't react that way again?"

"You can, because I don't want to experience that kind of misery again." He took her hand. "Can we start over?"

She thought of what he must have felt discovering his fiancée's deception and squeezed his fingers. "It's best we begin where we left off…right after you kissed me."

# Chapter 5

"I shouldn't have made it that easy for him," Kisha said to herself, sitting beside Craig as he drove her home in his car. He parked in front of the building in which she lived, got out and opened the door for her.

"These past weeks did some serious damage," he said as they approached her door. "I want more than anything to hold you, but I sense that you don't want that."

"You're right. My head and my heart are not in sync, and when that happens, my head wins. Let's give the wounds time to heal."

"I was so deeply involved with my own feelings that I didn't consider how you would feel."

She gazed into grim eyes and sheltered her own so that he wouldn't read in them her yearning to hold and comfort him. "Let's try to get over this," she said. "If we can't, well…we can't." Because she needed to touch him, she stroked his cheek with the back of her hand. Then she opened her door, looked past his shoulder and said, "Bye." It was either that or open her arms, and she wasn't about to embrace him.

Craig wasn't a man to hang his head or to mope, but the chill of their parting hit him where it hurt. If anyone had told him that he cared so much for her, he would not have believed it. He figured that he could make amends, but her distance was a lesson he would never forget. At home, he heated up a frozen pizza, got a bottle of beer and turned on the TV for company while he ate his dinner. The public broadcast station's report on projects for poor children did nothing to alter his mood, though his program of free music classes for some poor children and Kisha's free dental service to young children of low-income families were among those showcased.

He wondered if and when he'd find another woman who suited him better than she seemed to. They liked many of the same things, both had a streak of humanitarianism and their mutual physical attraction had to be obvious to anyone who saw them together. He drained the bottle and leaned back against the couch with his hands clasped behind his head. He had to get to know her better, and he needed to share himself with her. The memory of Judith's treachery no longer caused him pain; it made him feel like a fool. Could he let himself go with Kisha? Considering his feelings, did he have a choice? He phoned her.

"Hello, Kisha," he said when she answered. He hated the formality. "I want to share something with you."

"What is it?"

"Well, it requires that you dress very warmly and that I meet you at your office tomorrow no later than five o'clock."

"You've piqued my curiosity. All right. I'll be ready when you get there. But what will you do about the six o'clock news?"

"I'll tape it at around three-thirty. Thank you for agreeing to spend some time with me, Kisha. I'm not happy with the way we parted this evening."

"Neither am I, Craig, but let's not push it. What will be, will be."

"Yeah, but if I want it to be to my liking, I have to work on it."

Her laughter floated to him through the wire, warming him. If she could laugh with him, she could forgive him. He looked at his watch. "I'm in for a long twenty-one-hour wait. Good night, sweetheart."

"Good night, hon."

He hung up slowly. Had she really said what he thought he heard? His hopes higher than they'd been in a month, he suddenly felt like working, went to his study and began research for his special report on the displacement of some citizens for the common good—if indeed that new highway could be called that. He worked half the night and didn't know when he'd felt so exhilarated.

Kisha assumed that when Craig said warm clothing, he meant precisely that, and she dressed that morning in a tweed pantsuit, cotton-knit shirt and riding boots, but carried a cashmere sweater, woolen cap, gloves and long johns in a shopping bag. When Craig arrived at her office, she was wearing all of it.

"I feel like a stuffed pepper," she said when she greeted him.

He looked around the reception room, saw that it was empty, as he'd hoped, and pressed a quick kiss to her lips. "I love stuffed peppers," he said. "Come on. We'd better hurry. I want you to enjoy this."

"I'm sure I will," she said, having decided that she forgave him for having doubted her. When he took her hand, she grasped his fingers, looked at him and smiled.

"You haven't asked where I'm taking you or what we're doing when we get there," he said.

"Why should I? I like pleasant surprises."

He took the expressway to Oriole Park and maneuvered through traffic and side streets to the Fells Point lookout. "I think we're just in time," he said, looking around at several cars parked nearby. He sat with her on a bench, handed her a foam cup, opened a thermos and filled their cups with hot coffee. "This will help to keep you warm." He put his free arm around her shoulder and nestled her close to him.

Suddenly, she realized why he'd brought her there. The sky began to change into a kaleidoscope of red, blue, gray and orange colors, and the sun glowed in a deep red as it began its final descent. She had never seen such beauty, as the orange seemed to change into red and the gray to blue, and in it all, the sun edged slowly to its nightly resting place. It slipped out of sight, leaving behind a maze of fiery reds, oranges, purples and yellows.

Kisha gasped in awe at the sight she beheld. "It's so…so beautiful. Oh, Craig. Thank you." Shaken, tears streamed down her cheeks, and she turned her face to his shoulder. "I've never seen anything like it. Thank you for sharing it with me. I wouldn't have missed it for anything."

He wiped her tears with his handkerchief. "I won't ask why you're crying, because I suspect you felt what I was feeling. I awakened yesterday thinking that you were lost to me and now I... Well, I know we haven't settled it and that it isn't perfect, but you're sitting here with my arm around you, and that means I have something to go on. It's already getting colder. Shall we go?"

They walked to the car arm in arm, and when they were inside, she said, "Let's try to get over the past three weeks, but I don't mean we should forget them. The next time either of us is tempted to doubt, let's find a way to ask for the facts."

"Right. That's the lesson I got from this, and it's one that I will not forget." He rubbed the tip of her nose with his index finger. "Want some more coffee?"

She shook her head. What she wanted was a kiss, an honest-to-goodness, from-the-heart kiss. That touching moment when the sun slipped out of sight and his arms tightened around her was still with her. She reached out and trailed her fingers down the side of his face.

"If that's all I can have, I'll take it."

"What do you mean, 'If that's all you can have'?" he said, in something akin to a growl. "If I've got anything you want, say the word or find some other way of letting me know, and it's yours."

"Do I have to spell it out for you?" she whispered and raised her arms to him.

He stared down at her, and as his brown eyes took on a turbulence that she knew signaled a rise in his libido, heat flashed through her and sent her blood racing to her loins. His lips brushed hers, then he parted her lips with the tip of his tongue. Her arms tightened around him and, at that moment, she knew she wanted all of him. He broke the kiss and stared into her face, clearly shaken.

"I'd better drive while I can. I haven't made out like this since my…college days." He kissed her eyes and her cheeks, turned the key in the ignition and left Fells Point. Half an hour later, he stood with her at her door with her key in his hand as he gazed down at her. She couldn't read either his demeanor or the message in his eyes. Finally, she said, "Do you want to come in?"

But he shook his head, albeit slowly and with seeming reluctance. "Yes, I want to, but I don't think the time is right for what I need, and I'm hardly in the mood for self-denial. I'll call you. Okay?"

She smiled. This was a different Craig, the true man without the public persona, but with the assuredness that he always wore with such grace and style. She wanted to see more of this Craig. Not thinking, she reached up, grasped the back of his head and parted her lips. He slid his tongue into her mouth, lifted her, pressed his body against hers. As if shocked out of a bad dream he pushed her away from him. "Sorry," he said, panting. "I didn't mean for that to happen, and certainly not in that way."

To her way of thinking, all he'd done was whet her appetite. "You going to call me tomorrow?"

"I'll call you when I get home. Thanks for spending these pleasant moments with me."

She wasn't the wisest when it came to men, but the one thing of which she was certain was that Craig Jackson wanted her badly. Why had he neglected to pursue what he wanted and at a time when he should have realized that he was nearing his goal? she wondered.

"Maybe I'm being melodramatic about this," she said to

herself, hung her coat in the foyer closet and headed for the kitchen. In the process of opening the refrigerator door, she stopped short. "He didn't even suggest that we have dinner together. Is he losing it or am I the one who's going bonkers?"

She put two eggs in water to boil and looked in the refrigerator for something to pair with them. She found about a half cup of leftover chicken salad and released a sigh of relief. A few minutes later, she put the eggs in the freezer to cool, took her place mat and place setting to the coffee table in the living room and sat on the sofa facing the television. After a few minutes of the evening news, she took her supper of chicken salad, deviled eggs, cherry tomatoes and whole wheat bread to the living room and prepared to enjoy her supper. The telephone rang, and she saw Craig's landline number in the caller ID window.

"Hi, Craig, are you home already?"

"Yeah, I was just about to eat, when I realized that we could have eaten together. What must you think of me?"

"I thought about that a couple of minutes ago, but I didn't have time to mull it over."

"Please don't. Experiencing that awesome beauty with you in my arms after fearing that I'd never be with you again was a mentally enervating and emotionally draining experience." She wondered why he suddenly laughed, until he said, "I thought I was holding my own until you kissed me there at your door. Hmm. I guess we'd best leave that alone. Will you let me make up for my lapse and have dinner with me tomorrow evening. It'll take me about thirty-five minutes to get from the station to your house."

"I'd love it. Don't break the speed limit getting here."

"No danger of that, considering what the traffic will be like on a Friday evening. I'm looking forward to being with you."

"Me, too."

"Do you mean that?"

"I mean it."

With two root canals, some front teeth that needed caps and a wisdom tooth that required extraction, Kisha didn't have time to daydream about the coming evening with Craig. However, it was never far from her thoughts, and she managed to finish work at four o'clock. When Craig arrived at her house shortly after seven-thirty, she had the appearance of a woman who'd done nothing all day but loll around waiting for her date to arrive.

He greeted her with a kiss on the lips, which was both firm and possessive. The kiss was typical of the self-assured Craig she'd come to know. "You're so beautiful," he said. "I like the way you look in these reds and pinks. I'd love to take you and just run away with you."

"Who's stopping you?" she asked in a low, dulcet voice.

His facial expression said, "Keep that up and we might not get any dinner." Quickly, she moved past him, got her coat from the closet and handed it to him. Sparkles danced in his eyes, and laughter poured out of him, cutting the tension.

"What's so amusing?" she asked, in a voice much less seductive than it had been minutes earlier.

"I don't suppose you noticed that I have only two hands, and one of them is holding a bunch of flowers. What am I supposed to do with the coat you handed me in the hope that putting it on and marching out of here would get you out of trouble?" He kissed her nose.

She looked at the flowers, seeing them for the first time,

though she'd been vaguely aware that he was holding something. "They're so beautiful." She put the vase on her dining-room table. "I've always loved calla lilies, and I'm going to carry them at my wedding," she said, ignoring his remark. "Thank you."

"You're supposed to carry the flowers that your groom gives you," he said.

She brought another laugh from Craig when she poked out her bottom lip. "I'll tell him to give me white calla lilies."

He held her coat, hugged her and said, "Let's go."

"You don't have to take me to the most expensive places in Baltimore every time we go to dinner," she said after they finished an enjoyable meal in what looked to her like a palace.

"Only the best for my best girl," he said, almost airily as they approached his car nearly a block from the restaurant.

She stamped her foot, something she didn't remember having done since she was sixteen and her parents punished her for doing it. But she was unremorseful. "Thank you for saying I'm the best, but exactly how many 'girls' do you have?"

He blocked her entrance to the car, wrapped his arms around her and kissed her. "You never said you'd be my girl."

"You never asked me to be. You only wanted to know if any other man thought I was *his* girl."

He helped her into the car, got into his seat, closed the door and looked at her. "I see that was a mistake. Will you be my girl?"

"I wasn't asking you to ask me."

"I know, but it's the relationship that I want with you. Will you?"

"You've been treating me as if I was, so let's not change anything."

Craig leaned back against the seat and hooted. "Woman, it will not kill you to say yes at least once in your life. Are you my girl?"

"Uh-huh." She slid closer to him and rested her head against his shoulder. "If it wasn't so chilly, we could go bike riding one day. Maybe Sunday."

He leaned down, kissed her and started the car. "What time would you like to go bike riding Sunday?"

"Around eleven, okay?"

"Fine, I'll be there. If you don't have a helmet, I'll rent one. Be sure to dress warmly and wear thick gloves. It's early. Would you like to stop by Parkens Comedy Club?"

"Okay. Even if the jokes are lousy, I'll enjoy your company."

They spent an hour at the famous nightclub, and at times, she laughed almost uncontrollably. "I wish I knew why redneck jokes make me laugh and Uncle Tom jokes annoy me," she said as they left the club.

"Probably something to do either with racial attitude, self-consciousness, empathy for poor blacks or all three. Don't beat yourself up about it."

Kisha and Craig cycled through Grabill Park that Sunday morning and went canoeing there in the afternoon. They dined together three times during that week, and each time he left her at her door, their passion escalated. After he left her Friday evening, she vowed to bring their relationship to a head, but when she looked at the situation with clarity and honesty, she saw herself as the deterrent. After examining her thoughts and feelings, she realized that his three-week silence had continued to bother her.

The reasons he gave her made sense, but not entirely.

She snapped her finger. Craig was jealous, but he wouldn't admit it, not even to himself. The realization was the incentive she needed to take their relationship to the next level. Remembering how he enjoyed the floating island, the dessert they shared early in their relationship, she phoned him after he left her Saturday.

"Hi, Craig. How about coming over for supper tomorrow at about seven? I'm a reasonably good cook, so you won't have to find a restaurant after you leave."

"I'd love it. I'll be absolutely delighted. Thanks for asking me. Do you want me to bring anything?"

"Only your wonderful self," she said, and wondered if she hadn't been more effusive than was warranted. Well, he was wonderful, and she doubted that that little bit of praise would turn Craig Jackson into a fool.

"I wonder what she's up to now," Craig said to himself. Well, he'd enjoy seeing how she lived and the kind of woman she was at home, although he didn't anticipate any surprises. Such a feminine woman as Kisha would create a warm and welcoming environment for herself. During the last two weeks, their relationship had progressed better than he would have expected, considering their history. They needed a resolution, a consummation of what they felt for each other, and he intended to do all within his power to bring it about when he believed she was ready for it.

He arrived at Kisha's home that evening prepared for whatever came, or so he thought. One look at her in a red jersey halter dress when she opened the door, and he nearly dropped the flowers and wine that he held in his hands. She put his gifts on the table in the foyer, turned to him and opened her arms. When his arms went around her, the touch of his hands on her bare flesh startled him, and he stepped back.

"What's the matter?" she asked.

"Hi. It isn't every day that I get my hands on your bare flesh. Next time, warn me."

"Thanks for the flowers," she said of the multicolored lilies. Ignoring his comment, she added, "Oh, these are exquisite. Come on in. I'll put the wine in the refrigerator."

He followed her to the kitchen, mainly because any red-blooded man, seeing what he saw as she walked in front of him, would automatically have followed her. As she reached the kitchen door, she swung around.

"I don't mind your coming into the kitchen, but I don't want you to know what we'll be eating. Not yet, anyhow." She reached up and patted his cheek, "So go sit in the living room till I get there."

"Yes, ma'am." Without the fluid movements of her body to distract him, he noticed the paintings hanging on the walls of the hallway leading to the living room. Renditions of senior citizens, some frazzled, others serene, and of children at play adorned one side of the hall. On the other side hung paintings of outdoor scenes representing all four seasons. He liked the autumn scene best, for it captured the profusion of fall colors for which New England was famous. The signatures were penned by someone who could barely write. He sat on the sofa and looked around at the living room furnishings.

He would have expected a huge Persian carpet in the living room, but instead she had placed several seating groups near the fireplace on carpets of appropriate size to create a warm and hospitable environment. The words, *I could live with this woman* flashed through his mind, and he didn't question them.

"What would you like to drink," she asked, surprising him because he hadn't heard her enter the room. She placed a tray of hot hors d'oeuvres on the coffee table in front of him. "I've fixed a substantial meal, so feel free to have a drink or two."

"Thank you, but if we're having wine with dinner, I'll stick to one drink. I'm driving. I'll have a Scotch whisky and water or club soda please," he said.

She brought the drink and a glass of white wine for herself, and he liked what he saw when she glided around the place. Those movements had begun to rev up his desire.

"To you," she said after she sat down and raised her glass.

"To us. These things are scrumptious," he said of the tiny sesame-seed biscuits, cheese puffs and miniature quiches. I could make a meal off them and be more than satisfied. Who makes them?"

"I do," she said. "I like to cook."

He knew that he appeared taken aback. "Really? Well, if this is any indication of your skills, I won't eat any more of these. Would you please wrap a few of them up for me?" She wrapped them in foil, put them in a small shopping bag and put the bag on the table in the foyer.

"That way you won't forget them," she said, explaining what she'd done.

"Don't worry about that, sweetheart. I wouldn't forget anything that tastes that great."

She served a six-course gourmet meal and topped it off with a perfect floating island dessert. "Damn woman," he said, when she brought it to the table. "Are you trying to seduce me to putty."

The woman winked at him. "Well, I wouldn't say, 'to putty,' but…"

After two cups of espresso, which they drank in the living room, he stood and asked her, "Do you mind if I remove my jacket?" She said she didn't. "Any woman who cooks like you do should never have to do the dishes. I know my way around a kitchen, so I'll find what I need. You sit where you are." He leaned over, kissed her forehead and headed for the kitchen.

Kisha liked his mood, but she didn't see the need to comply with his order. So she went to the guest toilet downstairs, brushed her teeth, freshened up, and when he returned, he found her as he left her.

She patted the space beside her.

Craig sat down in the place indicated and looked at her. "Thanks for the invitation, but I certainly wasn't planning to sit across the room."

"Just making certain."

To her mind, things were moving too slowly. She couldn't offer more drinks, because if she drank more she'd be tanked, and that didn't fit with what she had in mind. She made as if to get up. "How about some music? I've got Billie Holiday recordings, and—"

He interrupted her, grasping her hand to detain her. "Are you nervous?"

"Uh…no. Of course not."

She could feel his arm snaking around her waist, almost like a slow tango. "After a meal like that one in an environment like this with a special person, a man needs his woman in his arms, wouldn't you think?"

She patted his knee. "What men want and why they want it are questions to which I have yet to find answers."

He tugged her closer to him. "You don't need to have the answer for men in general. You only have to understand *me*."

"If I had to take a test on that tomorrow," she said in what seemed to her like a gloomy note, "I'm not sure I'd pass."

"I suspect you'd do much better than you think you would."

This was getting too serious. She glanced up at him, tried to smile and failed. Every time she attempted to learn more about him, he clammed up. "I wish I did," she said.

When both of his arms enveloped her, she snuggled as close as possible to him. He tipped up her chin and gazed down into her eyes. She refused to hide what she felt for him. It was there, open, bare and bold, and she wasn't ashamed of it. Something flickered in his expression, and his lips trembled.

"I care deeply for you, Kisha, and I…I want you for myself, for me alone. Do you know what I'm saying?"

"I thought we had that settled," she said.

He stroked her arm. "You and I haven't settled anything, but we will."

"When?"

With his lips poised an inch above hers, he said, "Now. Right now," and claimed her mouth, demanding that she open to him and take him. She sucked his tongue into her mouth, intending to have her way with it, but he served notice at once that he was in charge of the moment. He probed his tongue in every crevice of her mouth until he'd heated her nearly to the boiling point. She crossed her legs in frustration as he caressed her bare back.

She felt his fingers at the buttons near her nape that held up her dress. "I've been looking at your beautiful breasts all night, and I want one of them in my mouth."

No more than she did. "You have to unbutton two buttons," she said. He managed it quickly, and as she arched her back in anticipation, he sucked a nipple into his mouth and began to suckle her as moans poured out of her. As if to increase her pleasure, she held his head. He suckled one breast and pinched and squeezed the other until, with the top of the dress pooled around her hips, she straddled him. She felt the bulge of his sex against her. This time, he would be hers.

Not wanting him to have time to think, she said, "The bedroom is upstairs." He didn't hesitate, and in minutes he had her flat on her back in her bed, wearing only her red bikini panties. He stripped off his clothes and pulled her to the edge of the foot of the bed. "May I pull these off you," he said as he tugged at her panties.

She lifted her hips, while Craig took them off and threw them over his shoulder. He parted her legs and kissed her. The sensation of his tongue probing her brought a scream from her very depth. He'd found the spot, and he teased and tantalized her until she'd thought she go insane.

"Honey, please let me have it. If you keep this up, I'll climax before you get inside me."

He stopped and looked at her. "Don't you like it?"

"I love it. I never felt anything like it."

He hooked her knees over his shoulder and sucked her clitoris until her screams pierced the room. "Please," she begged as the contractions in her vagina grew tighter. He quickly altered his onslaught and began kissing his way up her body.

"Look at me, sweetheart. Open your eyes and look at me. Take me in."

Staring into his eyes, she positioned him to enter her.

He sheathed himself to protect her. Then, shivers seemed to streak throughout her body when his penis touched her. She raised her hips and, after hesitating a moment, he sank into her. He put his hand between them and stroked her until she felt again that rush of heat at the bottom of her feet. He began to move slowly at first but as soon as she caught his rhythm, he began to drive with powerful strokes.

"Am I in the right place? Do you feel it? Tell me. Is it good for you, baby?"

She raised her body up to him. "Yes. Yes. Just like that. Yessssssss! She thought she'd die from the feeling. Then he seemed to hurl her higher and drop her down again. "Honey, I'm… I can't stand it. I'm dying." At last she could breathe, her thighs stopped quaking, and her body went still. He increased the power of his thrusts until he shouted his release and splintered in her arms.

After a long silence, he looked down into her face. "I take what we've just experienced as mutual commitment. I've never had this feeling of completeness before. I'm in this with you, Kisha. Do you care for me?"

"You know I do. If I didn't, you wouldn't be here. Yes, I care for you."

A grin spread over his face. "I'd begun to think you didn't know that word. It's the first time I ever heard you use the word *yes.*"

"Is not. I said it earlier when…well, you know."

His radiant smile seemed to envelop her. "Nothing said during sex, when you're out of control, counts."

"I wasn't out of control," she said, pouting.

"Oh, really?" His arms tightened around her, and his lips brushed hers, softly as if he cherished her, and he gazed down at her, smiling, occasionally kissing her cheeks, or her eyes, or the tip of her nose. Kisha felt cherished and loved. But she knew that there remained a part of him that he didn't release, and she also knew that, if she questioned him, she risked destroying the moment of oneness with him. So she saved her questions and her doubts for another time.

"Do you really care for me?" he asked her, his gaze fixed on her face. "Until those awful days when I thought it was over between us, I didn't realize how much I needed you."

"You're in my heart," she said, and paused as if searching for precisely the right word. "But if you want to stay there, Craig, you have to believe in me like I believe in you."

"Have no doubt of that," he said. "I'm not making that mistake again." She moved beneath him, surprising him, but he quickly recovered and drove them both to ecstasy. When she finally climbed down from the clouds into which he had thrust her, she told herself not to cry. It would last. It had to.

# Chapter 6

Later that night, Craig lay awake in his own bed thinking of what he experienced with Kisha. Suddenly he sat up, turned on the light, got up and walked to the window. He looked out at the cold night with its nearly bare trees and the city lights that seemed to twinkle like stars. Unable to shake the loneliness that had descended upon him the minute he'd left Kisha's bed, he put on a robe, went to the kitchen for a cup of instant coffee, took it to the living room and sat down. She'd changed him that night, and if he denied it, he'd be a liar. Wrapped in her arms, he knew at last who he was. For the first time in his life, he knew his potential as a man. He could not, and he would not let her get away from him. It was that simple. He believed she cared for him, and he was positive that he'd satisfied her, but he sensed a reticence or at least some reserve on her part. If he wanted Kisha

Moran for himself alone, he'd have to act boldly because winning her love wasn't going to be easy.

Kisha's euphoria was short-lived. Though enormously satisfying physically, her first lovemaking with Craig was not completely fulfilling. Almost as soon as he left her, she had a feeling of emptiness, as if she'd made love with someone she didn't really know. She didn't have that toasty, mushy feeling that women talked about and that she'd been led to expect after the earth-shattering loving she experienced with Craig. Still, she felt closer to him and cared more deeply for him than before they made love. But she wanted to feel as if they belonged to each other, and at that moment she didn't.

His phone call awakened her Monday morning. "Hello," she mumbled.

"Hi, sweetheart. I thought you'd be headed out of your door about now. Have you overslept?"

"I don't know. What time is it?"

"Eight twenty-six."

"Good Lord. I should be leaving home right now."

"Hold on. You're the boss, and if you're half an hour late, nobody's going to fire you. Take a deep breath. Getting stressed out the first thing Monday morning is bad for the nerves."

"I know. I didn't even hear my alarm clock. Craig?"

"You wound me. But if I'm the reason why you slept that soundly, I'll preen for a week."

She was fully awake now. "Well, spread your peacock plumes, hon. You're the culprit, because I do not oversleep. Here's a kiss and a hug. Call me later."

"Can we meet for lunch? I…I need to see you."

"Call me at eleven-thirty, and I'll tell you whether it's possible. I wouldn't mind seeing you, either."

His laughter, low and seductive, floated to her through the wires, warming her and filling her with anticipation. "I'm definitely glad to know that. See you later, sweetheart."

She took a fast shower, phoned for a taxi, dressed and made it to work by twenty minutes after nine. "I was getting worried," Regine, her receptionist, said when she rushed into her office. "But you look as if you just won the megamillion jackpot. You're just glowing."

"Must be the crisp air," she said, more embarrassed than she could remember ever being. "What's on the schedule for this morning."

"I wish the crisp air would make me look like that. Let's see. Mr. Tate wants his teeth brightened. Norma Creek thinks her braces should be adjusted, and Leon Rich wants you to do something about his halitosis. At three o'clock, you have Lena Smith for a wisdom tooth extraction."

She considered that an easy schedule, and unless a patient came in during the morning with an emergency, she could have lunch with Craig. When she walked into her workroom, Tate was already in the chair.

"Good morning, Doc. At least this isn't going to hurt. It's the first time I've looked forward to seeing a dentist."

"Good morning. Sorry I'm late, but I overslept. Don't expect your teeth to look as if you're six years old, Mr. Tate, and especially not after one treatment. If you'd quit smoking, they wouldn't be so yellow. Imagine what you're doing to your lungs. I'll do the best I can." An hour and a half later, she handed him a mirror. "That's the best for now. Any more and we'd risking losing some enamel. All right?"

"This is great. I didn't think it would look this good. By

the way, do you still give free service to poor kids one evening a week?"

"Yes. Why?"

He handed her a check. "That's wonderful work. Use this for some kids who need braces. I'm gonna try to quit smoking."

She thanked him. After he went to the receptionist's office, she looked at the check and gasped. Five thousand dollars. She stared at it for a full minute, wondering how that man guessed that she had to spend a sizable amount of her income in order to care properly for many of the children. She raced to the reception room to thank him again, but he'd left. The next patient would have to wait. She sat down, composed a handwritten thank-you note to the man.

"Regine, would you please address this to Mr. Tate and mail it today. Thanks."

"Will do. Do you want an eleven-thirty appointment today? I told the patient I'd call back."

"If it's one of my patients and an emergency, I'll take it. Otherwise I'm going to keep a personal appointment."

"It was neither. You can keep your date."

Adjusting the braces took only half an hour, so it delighted her that Leon Rich arrived early. You wouldn't have to pay me for this if you would do as I told you," she said to him when she'd finished. "I gave you a tongue sweeper. Use it when you brush your teeth."

He thanked her and left, but a minute later, he was back in her workroom. "What's this, Doc? She charged me a hundred dollars."

Kisha didn't bat an eyelash. "That's what I told her to charge you. I gave you a tongue sweeper for which I paid six dollars, but you won't use it. Forty-five minutes of my time is worth more than a hundred dollars, but I was easy on you. Using that sweeper won't cost you a penny."

"All right. All right, Doc. I get the message. We still friends?"

"Absolutely. And thanks for coming in on time."

She took off her white coat, refreshed her hair and makeup and telephoned Craig. "Where do you want us to meet?"

"If you're ready, I'll pick you up in ten minutes if traffic allows. Okay?"

"You can't park, so I'll be at the front door."

She wondered how much sense her rage to see him made. He'd left her barely eight hours earlier. Hopefully, she wouldn't have that empty feeling she'd gotten recently whenever they separated.

The white-and-blue taxi stopped in front of the building, and her heart began to race as he opened the door and stepped out. She dashed out of the building's revolving door and into his arms, and his startled expression caused her to wonder if she'd revealed too much of her feelings. But as she studied him across the small table in the cozy restaurant that he chose, she decided that if he didn't care a lot for her, his performance deserved an Academy Award.

"Could we share a meal this evening or see a movie or…or whatever, Kisha? I just…need to be with you." He punished his scalp as his fingers plowed through his hair. "If you say no, I'll understand and I'll accept it, but I… Kisha, is this normal?"

"Is what normal?"

"This… I want to be with you every minute."

"I don't know. I've only had limited experience with… with this stuff. At least you don't use any sharp instruments on people. I have to do surgery when I get back to my office."

"You're more than up to the task. Does that mean I can kiss you when I take you back?"

Her fork clattered against the plate. "Where would you do that?"

"In the taxi, of course. Didn't you ever make out in a taxi?"

"If by making out, you mean petting, sure, but not all that much."

"Too bad," he said, his expression almost as serious as if he were in deep mourning. "I'll do what I can to help make up for your lack of experience."

She stared at him for a moment, seeing the twinkle in his eyes that betrayed his attempt at seriousness. "You phony. For a minute, I was afraid that you really planned to take us back to our teenage years. Oh, Craig. I wish I'd known you then."

"Why?"

"I would have shared so much more of my life with you. That's why." She patted his hand. "I'll call you after I finish an extraction and let you know whether I'm in any shape to enjoy a few hours with you. That patient has teeth with roots as long as any I've ever seen, and he's more afraid of a needle than you are. If I'm lucky, I'll call you at about four-thirty. I know you'll be busy at that time, so I'll leave a message on your cell phone. Okay?"

"That'll be great. If your message is positive, I'll be at your place at seven-thirty. You can decide what we'll do."

When she left him, she walked into her building on shaky legs and slumped against the wall of the elevator, grateful that she was the only passenger. Craig Jackson had kissed her in that taxi as if he wouldn't have another chance.

She made her way into her office and collapsed into a chair. What had he done to her? She sat forward. There it was again, the sudden feeling of emptiness, the awful letdown. The loneliness. Seconds earlier, her euphoria was so encompassing that she had thought she'd fly.

"I can't stand it," she said to herself. "Why can't I feel as if we belong to each other?" Maybe it was her, but she didn't think so. She jumped up and snapped her finger as understanding dawned on her, and she vowed to discuss her thoughts with Craig. If, in doing so, she drove a wedge between them, so be it.

She wasn't sure that seeing Craig that evening was a good idea. She knew that when he took her home, they would repeat the scene in the taxi that afternoon. If that happened, they would make love again, and she didn't want that. However, her heart ignored her head, and she left a message on his cell phone that she would expect him at seven-thirty as agreed.

Craig finished the six o'clock newscast and dashed home to shower, dress and prepare himself mentally for a pleasant evening with the woman who had come to mean everything to him. She, or something, kept them from getting as close as he wanted them to be. He didn't doubt that she cared, and no man could expect a warmer, more complete response from a woman than he got from her. Yet, he'd swear that she kept a little space between them. Not when he had her in his arms. On those occasions, she capitulated totally, but at other times, in the tug of war between her heart and her head, her head ruled.

He put on a gray, pin-striped suit, light gray shirt and yellow tie, splashed on some cologne, got into his car and headed for Kisha's house. His cell phone rang and, seeing his mother's caller ID, he pulled over to the curb.

"Hi, Mom. What's up?"

"Nothing special. I'll be Christmas shopping tomorrow, and I can't decide whether to buy your father a laptop or a big flat-screen TV."

"How often would he watch television?"

"Not very often."

"There's your answer. I'm on my way to keep an appointment. May I call you tomorrow?"

"Hmm. Tomorrow, huh? Of course. Give her my love."

"Why do you think—"

She interrupted him. "Because your voice is filled with excitement. Have a lovely evening."

"Thanks. Give my love to Dad." He hung up. When had he become so transparent? With a quick shrug, he moved away from the curb and continued to Kelway Road, turned left and, within a few minutes, he rang Kisha's doorbell.

"Hi."

He gazed down at her, thinking how easily she tied him in knots. "Hello, sweetheart. How do you manage to be more beautiful each time I see you?"

"It's all… Let's go. I got us tickets to Buddy Guy. We can't eat popcorn, but we can hold hands."

"That's wonderful. Now what was it that you didn't say? It's all…what?" He held out his hand. "May I have the tickets, please?" He looked at them, opened his wallet and gave her fifty-six dollars. "Some good blues is exactly what I need. I had a difficult afternoon at the station."

"I hope it isn't serious," she said with a quizzical expression.

"I can handle it. It's all… What didn't you say?"

She turned and faced him, and even from his peripheral vision, he saw her testiness before she opened her mouth. "I didn't finish it, because I decided that it didn't apply to you."

"Really?"

"Absolutely," she said.

Buddy Guy was at his genius-level best, and with his woman beside him enjoying the music that he loved, all seemed right in his world. They had reached her house before he became conscious of the fact that she hadn't said a word during the ride home. At her door, he held out his hand for her key, opened the door, handed her the key and looked into her eyes. "May I come in?"

For an answer, she walked in, flicked on the foyer light and held out her hand to him. He tried without success to read her mood. Then she gazed up at him, her eyes wide and innocent and with a look of helplessness that belied everything he knew about her. "Don't you want me to stay?" The words came out in a whisper.

She stared at him, and a frown, which he later realized spelled confusion, crept over her face. "You know I do."

Her arms opened and, zombielike, he went into them. Home, where he belonged. She cupped his face with both of her hands, parted her lips and he plunged between them. He didn't know if he'd planned a scene with the blazing hot passion they'd experienced earlier. But when she rocked against him, sucking his tongue deeper into her mouth and letting her hands roam over his body, his blood raced hot and fast to his loins, singeing him, torturing his libido until she claimed him down deep where he lived. Resting hard and ready against her belly, he tried to pull away from her, but she wouldn't release him.

"Baby, something's got to give. I need to get in you so badly. If you want me to leave, please say so now."

She sucked in her breath. "You would leave me here like…like this?"

He lifted her from the floor and let her feel his readiness. "Can we… Do you want to be with me?"

When she loosened his tie and began to unbutton his shirt, he wanted to run with her. Minutes later he had her nude on her bed and stood over her stripping himself. Every second seemed like an hour. He thought he'd die if he didn't get into her. He lifted the sheet as if to join her, but she slid away.

"Lie down on your back, please."

Stunned, since she hadn't been an aggressive lover the previous night, he did as she asked, all the while praying that she didn't plan for them to have a verbal conversation.

Kisha didn't keep him guessing about her move. She leaned over him, brushed his lips with hers as she rubbed her flat left palm over his right pectoral. Evidently getting the reaction she wanted, she eased her left leg across his body just below his belly, parted her lips over his mouth and pulled his tongue into her mouth.

With her nipples grazing his chest and her pubic hair brushing below his belly, was she deliberately punishing him? He bucked beneath her in an attempt to suck one of her nipples into his mouth, but she slipped downward and twirled her tongue around his pectoral. Sensations plowed through him, and he thought his nerves had twisted into a knot.

"Sweetheart, this is… Baby, this is hell. I'm going out of my mind."

For a response, her warm tongue licked its way to his navel, and he nearly bucked off the bed when the tips of her fingers began to gently knead his testicles.

"What are you doing to me?" he groaned.

"No more than you did to me last night."

He shouted aloud when her hand stroked the underside of his penis. "Baby, I can't take much more of this."

"Yes you can. I'm just getting started." When she dragged her body to the foot of the bed, tracing her tongue from his navel downward, he braced himself. She wrapped her arms around his hips, and he held his breath. Her hot tongue circled the tip of his penis, and he grabbed the side of the bed and prayed for control.

"Oh, my God," he moaned, when she sucked it into her mouth. And then it seemed as if a storm was upon them, shaking him from head to foot in a turbulence he'd never known. She feasted on his penis with her tongue, lips and cheeks like a child lapping and sucking a sweet lollipop. His body wanted him to lie there and let her finish him, but he knew the danger of that. With all the willpower he possessed, he sat up and moved her from him.

"You were about to make me lose it, and I couldn't permit that," he said. She thwarted his effort to put her in the missionary position, eased him to his back, climbed on him and took him into her. Almost immediately, her climax began. He got her left nipple into his mouth and sucked the sweet thing until she cried out.

"Why won't it come? It's just teasing me."

"Be still, baby." He planted his feet firmly and stroked her with all the power he possessed until her screams split the air. Then he let himself go, as every muscle in his body quivered with his release. With his arms thrown wide, he gave himself to her as he'd never before given himself to a woman. He was hers, and he knew it.

When he could get his breath and collect his wits, he

opened his eyes and looked up at her, hoping to find in her what he felt within himself. "What you just gave me should amount to a commitment," he said. "Does it?"

She leaned forward, brushed his lips and then pressed her parted lips to his. If she was again evading a direct answer, he was having none of it. He flipped her over on her back and attacked first one of her erogenous places and then another, kissing her ears, neck, throat and the sides of her breasts until she moaned in protest.

"Why are you doing this? You know what I want," she said.

"No I don't. Show me."

He could almost feel her frustration, as she clasped the back of his head and pressed his lips to her nipple. He sucked it into his mouth and, within seconds, she began to writhe beneath him.

"I don't need all that. Just get in me."

"I will." He kissed his way to her belly, let his tongue frolic there and then moved slowly down, kissing the inside of her thighs, teasing her clitoris with his thumb while she swung her hips up to him in a plea for more. When he let her feel the warm pressure of his tongue, she cried out, but he was not in a mood to be merciful and possessed her until she exploded.

Then he kissed his way up her body, looked down at her and said, "Ah, love. Take me." She reached down and grasped him, locked him into her and let a smile float over her face as he began to thrust into her. In no time, her climax gripped him like a raging storm, wringing from him the essence of life. He braced himself on his elbows and collapsed in her arms. When he awakened more than an hour later, his first thought was that he didn't want to exist without her.

* * *

She wanted to commit to him, but how could she when she didn't have that feeling of oneness that she needed with him so desperately. He stirred, letting her know that he had awakened, and kissed the curve of her shoulder.

"Are you all right, sweetheart?"

"Physically, I definitely am."

He rolled off her and sat up. "But not emotionally? Is that what you're telling me?"

She'd vowed that the next time it happened, she'd tell him about it, because she didn't believe the fault rested solely with her. "I'm not quite sure how to put this, Craig, but what I need to say is terribly important."

"Try. I promise to listen with an open mind."

"More than that, Craig. I need you to listen with compassion, too. When I'm with you, like this afternoon and you kissed me until I hardly knew where I was, I was in heaven. And just now, when you were loving me, if you'd told me I owned the world, I would have believed it—"

"But?"

"But I walked into my office this afternoon, sat down and had this terribly empty, lost and deserted feeling, as if I'd just been with a stranger. The same thing happened the minute you left my bed last night. I did everything I could—remembered everything about you, everything you did to me—but I couldn't recapture that warm, loving feeling of oneness I knew when you had me in your arms.

"I came home this afternoon impatient for seven-thirty when you'd ring my doorbell, and yet I was scared to death that you'd make love to me, send me to the stratosphere and then I'd feel as I did when you rolled off me a minute ago. Craig, I care for you, but I realized this afternoon that I have this feeling of desolation because I don't know you."

"What do you mean, you don't know me?"

"I don't. I don't know your height, weight, what month you were born in, and a whole bunch of other intimate things about you. You said your parents live in Seattle, but have you ever lived there? And what about your parents? Are they old, young, alone or capable of caring for themselves. I know you love floating island dessert, but do you like biscuits and corn bread? Craig, honey, I need to feel a oneness with you, that I belong with you."

"And you don't. All right. I'm six feet three and an half inches tall. I weigh one ninety-two. I like biscuits, and I'm crazy about my mother's corn bread." He said it in a monotone and fell back on the bed. Nobody had to tell her that he hoped the subject was closed.

Craig fell back on the bed and closed his eyes. When he left her the previous night, he'd felt a loneliness of a kind that he hadn't previously known. Yet, it wasn't the sense of desertion that she seemed to have felt but hadn't articulated. It was knowing that he belonged with her and realizing that he hadn't laid the groundwork that would make being with her a reality. She needed a lot from him. But he had never been able to bare his soul to anyone, not even his mother. Did she want to see his insides? He guarded carefully information about his parents, mainly because he had to keep his private life separate from his public life. He shunned any person and anything that would make him fodder for supermarket tabloids. Further, he didn't want to benefit from his father's reputation as a famous attorney, nor did he want its backlash. He fought against a rising irritation.

She needed more than he'd given her, and she needed it right then, but he felt drained. What could he say to her that would bridge the chasm that he now felt as deeply as he knew she must. He found her hand and locked her fingers with his.

"Try not to feel as if I desert you, because I haven't and I never will. I'm trying to deal with what you've just said, but it will take some time. So cut me a little slack, and I promise we'll talk about this again. Will it upset you if I leave now? I need to think, and I'm not sure I can with you lying so close to me."

Her hand stroked the side of his face, barely touching, in that way that always made him feel treasured. "Do you…want more for us?"

He sat up and turned to her. "I've noticed your reticence, subtle though it's been, to…well, accept me fully. Are you saying this is the reason?" Craig asked.

"I didn't know I was doing that, but if it's true, I suppose it's because I don't want to hurt. Like right now." He reached over, took her to him and held her. She seemed to soak up the comfort of his arms like a sponge taking in water. "You're only postponing it," she said.

"Perhaps. But I need this, too." He held her for more than an hour. Her breathing deepened, and when he realized that she was asleep, he slipped out of bed, dressed, pressed the automatic lock on her front door and left. He prayed that she would sleep until her alarm clock sounded.

Kisha turned over and stared at the ceiling, bereft at the feel of his hands slipping away from her body. She tried to imagine what she could do to bring him out of his secrecy. A sense of unease stole over her as it occurred to her that he didn't trust her. But why? She'd been honest and open with him. She slid out of bed and headed for the bathroom. As warm water showered her body, she rummaged through her mind for reasons that a man like Craig Jackson might be insecure and could find none. She'd give him some space. If he wanted her, he'd have to make some changes.

Craig finished his broadcast that Friday evening, took a taxi to the Baltimore-Washington Thurgood Marshall Airport and headed for New York City for a weekend of Christmas shopping for the men on his list and a chance to see an opera and a Broadway play. As usual, he shopped for the women on his list last, because he dreaded doing so. He registered at the Park Lane Hotel facing Central Park, walked two blocks down to Carnegie Hall on Fifty-Seventh Street and bought a ticket to the Cleveland Orchestra concert that had begun fifteen minutes earlier.

"It great to be back in this city," he said to a seat mate at intermission. "This is one place where you can get the best of everything."

"Don't I know," the older man said.

At the end of the concert, they left together, discovered that they were staying at the same hotel and agreed to have a late supper together. Upon learning that the man was a recent widow after sixty years of marriage, Craig decided to ask him a question that he'd planned to put to his father.

"Sir, you say you had a long marriage and a very good one. What makes a happy marriage?"

"Oh, that's simple," the old man said. "Trust and commitment. The hot stuff burns off after a while, and you have to deal with day-to-day living. That's when push comes to shove. If you're not in it for keeps, it'll tank like a balloon with a hole in it. But if you mean business, and she's there for you, you'll love each other more every day."

He thought about those words the next day when he was on his way to a matinee performance of *Rocking* a Broadway play. Crisp winter air invigorated him, and he walked with quick and purposeful steps down Seventh Avenue. The scent of roasting chestnuts greeted him, tempting him to find their purveyor. His gaze caught the window of a curio shop, and he stopped, ventured closer and stared. A strange happiness seemed to flow over him, and a smile covered his face. Glancing at his watch, he saw that he had twenty-six minutes before curtain time, so he walked in, approached a clerk and left the store minutes later carrying a gold-colored shopping bag.

At four-thirty, he left the theater, hailed a taxi and went to Bergdorf Goodman department store to shop for Christmas presents. His personal shopper greeted him as if he were a good friend. "I'm so glad to see you, Mr. Jackson," she said. "I have here your gift list and purchases last year and the year before. Would you care for some coffee?"

He did and she ordered coffee, sandwiches and petits fours, for which he was grateful, since his lunch consisted of a hot dog and a handful of peanuts, and he wouldn't have time to eat dinner before going to the opera. Within an hour and a half, he had three silk scarves, two sets of personalized handkerchiefs, a humidor engraved with the initials of the intended recipient, a brown leather toiletries case for his father, several leather wallets for various colleagues and a red silk tie for his boss.

"I'll see that these are delivered to your hotel by nine this evening," she told him, and he knew he could depend on it.

Craig thanked her, tipped her well, ducked out of the

Fifty-Eighth Street exit and went to his hotel. In his hotel room, he kicked off his shoes, threw his jacket across a chair, sat on the bed and dialed Kisha's number.

"Hello. I called you a few minutes ago, but you didn't answer. How are you?" Kisha said.

"Great. This morning I saw a collection of wonderful Rembrandts. This afternoon I saw a play, the best stress reliever imaginable, and I'm leaving the hotel in an hour for the Metropolitan Opera to see *Othello*.

"I didn't realize you were in New York. When you said you planned to do Christmas shopping, go to the museums and see a play, I wondered why you didn't ask me to go with you, but I didn't dwell on it. Everybody needs breathing space. I'm glad you're having a great time. When have you found time to eat?"

"So far, I haven't eaten at any of the spectacular restaurants here, but I don't mind. We have great restaurants in Baltimore."

"Have you done any shopping?"

"Yeah. I always go to Bergdorf's, and a personal shopper helps me with that, so it doesn't take long. I wish you'd been with me at the theater this afternoon. Well, we could do that one weekend. I have to dress, and getting a taxi at theater time can be difficult, so I'd better go. Can I have a kiss?" She made the sound of a kiss, and he returned it.

"Enjoy the opera."

"Thanks. I'll see you tomorrow afternoon."

He hung up and stared at his cell phone. Damn the opera. He wanted to see her, and he wanted to give her the little present he'd bought for her. "Self-control is a good and useful thing, even necessary," he said aloud, and told himself that it wouldn't kill him if he waited seventeen hours to see her.

# Chapter 7

When the plane on which he flew back to Baltimore landed, Craig reached for his cell phone and dialed Kisha's number. "My plane just touched down," he said when she answered. "I should knock on your door within ninety minutes at the latest, earlier if I can make it."

"Wonderful. I'll be right here. It's cold outside. I opened the door to get the paper, and that frigid wind almost blew me away. Are you going home first?"

"Hadn't planned to. Why?"

"Just checking. I can't wait to see you."

"Same here. The plane's at the gate, so I'll be kissing you soon."

"You say the nicest things. Bye for now."

An hour and twenty-five minutes later, he stepped into Kisha's house, dropped his overnight bag on the floor of her foyer, and pulled her into his arms. His only thought was getting her as close to him as possible, and he couldn't do that to his satisfaction. She stepped back from him with a quizzical expression on her face and, as if approving of what she saw, she stood on tiptoe, parted her lips and urged his mouth to hers. He hadn't wanted to kiss her, because he needed her so badly and he didn't want to give her the impression that he thought only of getting her in bed. Her kisses always sent him into a tailspin. He ended the kiss and hugged her.

"You're lethal," he said. "How about a glass of water?"

She looked at him as if she didn't believe what she heard. "You go in there and have a seat," she said, pointing toward the living room. "I'll be there in a couple of minutes." A few minutes later, she returned with coffee, vanilla ice cream, barely warm hot-cross buns and a glass of water. She put the tray on the coffee table, sat beside him and took his hand.

"Did you have a successful trip?"

"Absolutely. I did half of my Christmas shopping, saw a good play, an opera and a superb concert. Did you miss me?"

Her left hand stroked the side of his face. "Of course I did. You were gone three-quarters of the weekend."

He gave her the shopping bag that he'd placed on the floor between his feet. "I saw this, and I wanted you to have it."

While she stared at the curly, cream-coated baby lamb, his nerves began a slow shiver throughout his body. He didn't know how she'd take the gesture.

"What…what is it?" he asked, when tears clouded her eyes and slowly dampened her sweater. She wiped her eyes with the hem of the sweater.

"Kisha, what is it. Don't you like it?" She shook her head from side to side as the tears gushed from her eyes. Thinking that he had upset her with the gift, which was obviously a child's toy, he attempted to retrieve it, but she held on to it. "Sweetheart, the last thing I wanted was to upset you. I saw it, and it looked…so warm and…I thought of you."

He put his arms around her and rocked her.

She held the little lamb to her breast, then kissed its nose. "It's the most precious thing anyone ever gave me," she said, hugging and kissing the furry toy. "I'm going to name him Bingo." She slid her arms around Craig's neck, kissing and hugging him. "I'm going to keep Bingo as long as I live."

"You really like it?"

"Oh, Craig. This tells me how you really feel about me and that you were thinking of me. I love him. And it's a he, not an it."

At last he could laugh. A few minutes earlier, he'd been afraid that he'd hurt her. "I have a lot to learn about you, Kisha. For all your sophistication, you're down to earth. I realize that you like simplicity and simple things. That suits me." He began to stand. "Mind if I warm this hot-cross bun and this coffee?"

She stood. "I'll do it." After she left him, he looked around for the little lamb, but she had carried it with her. He had just gotten an important clue about his new girl-friend. Little things mattered more to Kisha than flashy restaurants and expensive gifts. He wouldn't forget it.

He got up, followed her into the kitchen and locked his arms around her. "It's strange, but you just left me, and I was…" He hesitated, not wanting to expose too much of himself. "I didn't want you to be away from me." After they held each other for a minute, he pulled a straight-back chair from the table, straddled it and sat down.

"I hadn't planned to spend the remainder of the day with you. If I were smart or sensible, I'd go home and work on a special broadcast that I'm planning for this coming Thursday. But that idea just went out the window. Could we have dinner together this evening?"

"If you're sure you don't want to work, I'd like it very much." She kissed the little lamb and put it on the table. "Sure you won't be sorry you didn't work on your project?"

"Trust me, it won't be a problem."

He carried the tray of hot-cross buns and coffee to the living room and put it on the table beside a recliner, sat down and stretched out his legs. He patted his knee, and she sat on his lap and relaxed against him. "I could stay this way with you forever," he said, reached for the remote control and flipped on the radio. With the soft sound of instrumental guitars and strings surrounding them, they ate the buns, drank the coffee and wordlessly let love envelop them.

Hours later, Kisha awoke in a darkened room, realized that she'd been asleep in Craig's arms and attempted to get up from the recliner, but he detained her. "I wonder how long I slept. It's already dark."

"I don't know when I last napped in the daytime. It's six thirty-two, and I'm hungry. Should I make a dinner reservation or would you rather I call for takeout."

She stretched languorously, hugged him and then stood. "Neither. In half an hour, I can heat a can of New England clam chowder, defrost some leftover chili that I made, cook some rice and make a salad. You set the table, open some red wine, and we'll have a nice meal right here. What do you say?"

"I'd say no, but I love both chili and clam chowder."

"You fixed dinner, so I'll clean up," he said later after they finished eating. "If we'd gone to one of my favorite restaurants, I doubt I would have enjoyed the food as much as I enjoyed that chili. You wouldn't teach me how to make it, would you?"

"Hmm. If that's the secret to your heart, why should I give it away?"

"It isn't, and you already have the secret to my heart."

If he wanted to talk seriously, they would sit together and talk, but not when he was in the kitchen and she was walking toward the dining room. That way of giving her snatches of him was at the root of their problem, and even after she told him in plain English, he seemed not to have grasped it.

When he came back to her, she thought she detected a change in his demeanor. "I'd better go. This entire afternoon has been like a balm for my soul. I guess I needed some unstructured time with you. While you slept in my arms, you murmured my name. It meant more to me than anything you could have said. I want a lot from you right now, but I don't think it's appropriate."

She hardly knew what to make of that. "Craig, honey, it's always appropriate for us to level with each other."

He stared down at her. "I'm sure you're right." Standing there in her foyer, he shook his head several times. Then, he suddenly gripped her firmly to him, and kissed her. "If I made love with you tonight, neither of us would ever forget it. I'll call you when I get home." He picked up his weekend bag and left.

She stood there for a minute musing over his odd behavior. Then she locked the door, went to the kitchen and got the little lamb and climbed the stairs to her bedroom.

As she hugged the precious little lamb, she said aloud to herself, "God forbid that this should be all of Craig that I'm left with."

His call came as she was getting in bed. "Hi. Are you home safely?"

"Yes, but just barely. I escaped an out-of-control car by a hair. He finally hit a post and stopped. It seems that the driver wasn't badly hurt, but an ambulance took him to the hospital anyway."

"It must have shaken you."

"It was unnerving, but I'm fine. I hope that driver will be all right. Kisha, I enjoyed this afternoon with you more than any time we've spent together. I don't know why, but I... We were so close. I want to ask you something, but not over the phone. Can we meet for lunch tomorrow? I won't have time for more than a sandwich."

"In that case, why not come by my office around twelve-thirty, and I'll order us some crab cakes and lemonade."

"In that case, why don't I bring it? But it's too cold for lemonade. What about coffee?" She agreed. "I'll be there at twelve-thirty."

She sat in bed with her knees drawn up toward her chest and wrapped her hands across her legs. *What could he possibly want to ask her that was so important that he had to ask in person?*

If his request had confused Kisha in Craig's mind his intentions were clear. He belonged with Kisha, and after their strange, but satisfying afternoon together, he would never doubt it. He was hers completely and unequivocally, and if he had made love with her, she would have known that he was putty in her hands. Although he was practically certain that she loved him, he was not sure that she was content, not to speak of happy, to forget about other men and cast her lot with him. She was a woman whose mind wrestled continuously with her heart and her emotions, and he'd bet that her mind won at least half of the time.

He got a bottle of beer from the refrigerator, opened his computer and outlined the content of the special broadcast he'd promised his viewers for the coming Thursday.

The next morning, Monday, he arose early, revised the plan, printed it out and smiled. His boss, was going to love that broadcast.

He walked into Kisha's office at the appointed time and couldn't help laughing. He'd swear that his tooth began to hurt the minute he crossed the threshold. With a "table" already set on the desk in her office, she greeted him without her white coat and with her hair hanging loosely around her shoulders.

"Hi, sweetheart," he said and kissed her nose. "All I've had today is one doughnut and two cups of coffee, so I'm starving."

"I can see that," she said, staring at the six crab cake sandwiches, a green salad and two large peach cobblers, plus the coffee.

"You have a big appetite, Craig, but how can you eat all that?"

"Sweetheart, I'm a big man, and I exercise every morning. You don't like skinny men, do you?"

"If I did, what would you do?"

"Probably spend more time exercising, but I couldn't give up food. I love to eat." He dumped the remains of their lunch into a plastic shopping bag. "I'll dispose of this. You want to know what I have to discuss with you."

He pulled his chair to face hers and took both of her hands. "Our relationship is in limbo. We don't get closer, although we care for each other. I don't want to lose what we have. In fact, I want us to see if we can make a go of it. Will you…spend next weekend with me at my country place in Marriottsville? It's beautiful all year round, quiet and peaceful. You have questions about me and about us. Maybe we can find there what we need in each other." He released her hands and gripped her forearms. "I'm in deep here, Kisha. Will you give us a chance?"

His heart seemed to constrict when she looked away from him. "I also want more than we have, Craig, and I need more. But I don't think we're there yet. Yes, we're intellectually compatible and I couldn't ask for a sweeter, more satisfying lover, but something is missing. I tried to tell you about it, but I didn't succeed, and I can't settle for less than what I know I need. Maybe we shouldn't be in the kind of relationship you're suggesting.

"I promised myself that I wouldn't bring it up to you again. If it happens naturally, maybe we'll make it. If not, we'll go our separate ways. I won't be happy, but I need to give myself a chance."

If she'd shot him, the pain would have been easier to bear than what he felt at that moment. No woman had ever rejected him in such a manner. Cut-and-dried. He wasn't used to it. He looked at her for long minutes, but she looked him in the eye and waited for his response.

He pushed back anger. He cared for her and didn't want to end their relationship. But he didn't think he deserved her cold-hearted rejection. "I don't know how you define relationship," he said, gritting his teeth. "But any intelligent woman who knew what's happened between us would tell you that we are *in* a relationship, and deeply at that. We've made love, not once but twice, and on two consecutive evenings at that. Moreover, I didn't have to urge you. You wanted it as much as I did, and you made that clear to me. So I don't know where this is coming from. I deserve better."

"It happened in moments of weakness, and you knew you were doing it."

"Tell me you didn't enjoy making love to me, and I'll tell you you're lying."

She didn't respond, and she wouldn't, because he knew she had integrity. She wouldn't lie. Instead, she fought back.

"The trouble is that you wrap yourself up like a mummy and won't let anybody get next to you. I told you once that I have no idea who you are."

He stared at her. "Really! My name is Craig Jackson, only son of John Fentriss and Avery Jackson, both law-abiding citizens." He looked at his watch. "Look, I have to get back to my office. Think about the weekend."

"Yes. And I have a patient in twenty minutes. Thanks for the food."

He wasn't any good at pretense, so he didn't kiss her. She'd hurt him. "I'll call you."

"Okay," she said, but he noticed that she'd poked out her chin.

She hadn't meant her remarks to sound critical and un-feeling, the way they had, and she couldn't take them back. Besides, she'd spoken the truth. He'd told her the absolute minimum about his parents. Just their names. If he'd said Jane and John Doe, she wouldn't know any more or any less about him. And wasn't that the second time he'd done that? He was planning an important broadcast, but he didn't share with her a single word about its content or what it meant to his career. She put on her white coat, pinned up her hair, washed her hands and got ready to fit the caps on a pair of front teeth. One day soon, she'd have to decide what to do about her relationship with Craig Jackson.

When she got home, a message on her answering machine reminded her that, since her relationship with Craig heated up, she'd seen very little of Noreen, her next-door neighbor. She dialed the woman's number.

"Kisha, girl, where you been? I had my first real shoot today as representative of Dainty Diapers. You wouldn't believe how I looked. I didn't recognize myself. Come over, and I'll show you the pictures. I have a pot of greens cooking, I'm roasting a chicken and I can bake some sweet potatoes in the microwave oven. You coming?"

"Be there as soon as I change my clothes."

The minute Kisha stopped inside Noreen's home, her neighbor began interrogating her.

"That was one good-looking brother who showed up at your door yesterday afternoon. I mean, we're speaking *fine*. What was he doing bringing a suitcase? He staying with you?"

Kisha fastened her fists to her hips and frowned at her friend. "Do I look that stupid to you? I have no intention of being a convenience for any man. Where're those greens?"

"Follow your nose. We'll eat in a minute."

They finished eating, cleaned the kitchen and moved into the dining room where Noreen had spread out copies of the still photos that her sponsor planned to use for print advertising.

Kisha scrutinized the photos. "These are lovely, Noreen.

You're so glamorous. I won't be surprised if I see you starring in a movie."

"Me in a movie? Say, I saw some paintings in the company CEO's office the other day, and they didn't look to me to be any better than some I've seen you do. Of course, I'm no art expert, but why don't you find out if your work is any good."

"I don't think it's bad, but I don't have enough for a show."

"Oh, for Pete's sake. That's no excuse. Paint some more."

She loved to paint, and since she wasn't going to be seeing Craig any longer she'd have time in which to paint. On Saturdays, from sunup until sunset, she painted. It didn't take the place of a relationship with Craig, but it made being without him more bearable. She wanted to be with him or at least to talk with him on the telephone, but he'd said he would call. If he didn't call they wouldn't be together again, because she was determined not to make the first move.

Fate apparently had its own agenda. When Kisha arrived at her office the next morning, she saw Craig leaning against the door. "Déjà vu," she said with a grin as she unlocked the door.

"Tell me about it. It hurts like the devil."

Her eyebrows shot up. "Not the same tooth?"

"No. This one hasn't bothered me before, so maybe it won't be so bad and you can give me a pill for the pain."

"Have a seat in my chair. I'll be right with you."

"Does that mean you're going to be hard-hearted and give me a needle?"

She didn't answer, but walked back into the examining room with the needle in clear view. When he shrank from it, she couldn't help feeling sorry for him. She put the needle down.

"Open your mouth, please. I'm going to rub this pain-killer on your gum. Which tooth is it? Ah, yes." Now close your eyes and think pleasant thoughts." She rubbed the gel onto his gum. "Keep your eyes closed and trust me to make you as comfortable as possible."

"Why do you want me to close my eyes? The only pleasant thing about this is looking at you."

"Behave. You will relax more easily with your eyes closed. Open wide." She inserted the needle, and sweat beaded his forehead.

"I'm sorry, Craig. I know it hurts, but this time I don't think I have to do a root canal."

"It wasn't nearly as painful as I thought it would be," he said.

She looked into those eyes that she loved and smiled. She wanted to kiss him, but she wondered if a man with a half-numbed lip would be a very good kisser.

"I missed you, Kisha. I was so glad when this tooth started hurting, because it gave me a reason to see you."

"I'm not glad your tooth hurts, but I am grateful for it. This time, are you going to do the right thing and get follow-up care?" She took some pictures of his tooth.

"A grin spread over his face. I'll have to think about that. By the way, did you throw away that little lamb?"

"Are you serious? Bingo hangs out on my bed."

"I am definitely not going to touch that."

She looked at the pictures of the tooth. "You need a filling, so brace yourself for some drilling. It won't be too bad." She flipped on the radio. He clutched her hand.

"If you had my interest at heart, you'd sing to me."

Laughter poured out of her. "I can't sing while I'm drilling this tooth, and if you insist on talking, I'll never finish."

"Why can't you just kiss it and make it better."

"Why can't you just behave? This is a serious cavity, and if I don't do this properly, you'll really know what pain is."

"Okay, but promise to kiss me when you finish."

"I can't. I already thought of it, but you can't kiss a person whose lips are numb."

"Point taken. But at least you wanted to, so kiss me later when the stuff wears off. As soon as they feel normal, I'll come back, and you can—"

"Craig, You're nuts. Now stop talking and let me get this tooth cleaned out before the Novocain wears off and I have to give you another shot."

"Okay, I'll be quiet, but I've been miserable without you. Have you missed me at all?"

She leaned forward and kissed his cheek. "I…I missed you an awful lot, and I've been so annoyed with you for not calling me like you promised that I don't watch your newscast any more."

"When I left you that day, I was so hurt that I taped my newscast, drove to my place in Marriottsville and walked in the woods trying to figure out where I miscalculated." She let her gaze give him gentle censure. "All right. I'll be quiet. I've probably wrecked your appointments schedule for today."

He had, but she was so happy to see him and to mend their broken relationship that she'd gladly forgo lunch in order to catch up with her appointments. She finished drilling, put in the filling, patted his shoulder and told him he was as good as new.

"Thanks. But what about you and me? Are we as good as new?"

"Yes. I realize that I have to learn how to say what I think without sounding caustic and insensitive. And you have to try to…to be more open. That's not quite the word, but now you know what I mean."

He opened his arms, and her heart fluttered with joy as she went into them. "You belong here, Kisha. Right here in my arms."

"I know. Now scat so I can get to my next patient."

"I'll call you later."

It was more than he'd hoped for. So much more. He hadn't doubted that she would take care of his tooth and do her best, but he hadn't dared think that she would receive him as she did with warmth and the sweetness that made her so precious to him. When he saw her, his heart pained him as much as his tooth did, and one thing was instantly clear to him—he didn't want to live his life without her.

He took a cab back to his office at the station and dialed his father's number. "Attorney Jackson is engaged just now," the supercilious voice of his father's secretary advised him. She'd better pray that he got a national news program before March. If he joined his father, his first act would be to see that she got fired.

"Jillian, this is Craig. Would you get my father on the phone, please?"

"Yes, of course."

"Hi, Dad. The network bigwigs gave me high marks for my special program on single mothers and deadbeat dads. The network was flooded with calls. I did it for my local station, but a lot of satellite channels picked it up."

"Well, you're moving farther and farther from my

dream, but I'm proud of you, son. It's wonderful news. I've always known that you will succeed at whatever you do."

"Thanks, but sometimes that which means most to us is the most elusive."

"Whoa there. Are you telling me there's a girl you want who's giving you a hard time? What's her story?"

"She says I don't open up to her and that I'm wrapped as tight as a mummified Pharaoh."

"Well, I'll be! It might help to talk with your mother about that. When I was trying to get her to marry me, she accused me of that."

"You're kidding."

"Once you share yourself with that woman, you'll see a change in both of you. Women are nurturers, son. She needs to know what makes you happy, what you want in life and especially what hurts you. When I first started out, I lost a tough case. You can't imagine how that thing hurt, and how I dreaded telling your mother. One look at me and she knew it the minute I walked into the house. She smiled, opened her arms, and at that moment I felt as if I could throw a steer. Open up to this woman. If she loves you, you'll be a happier man. Bring her up here to meet us."

"Thanks. I'll ask her. See you soon."

"Right. And keep up the good work."

He mused over their conversation for a while. Since early childhood, his parents had taught him to shoulder his own load, and he hadn't wanted to disappointment them. So he'd grown accustomed to keeping a stiff upper lip when he hurt and not sharing his problems, concerns or weaknesses with others. He had regarded that level of sharing as baring one's soul, and he'd been embarrassed by anyone who did it in his presence. After his talk with his father, Craig realized that he would have to make some changes. He wouldn't allow Kisha to leave him because of his inability to open up. He would just have to find a way to share his feelings and himself.

Kisha sailed into her house that evening, turned up the thermostat, put her boots and coat into the foyer closet and considered ordering a take-out dinner from a local restaurant so that she could spend the evening painting. The phone rang and, almost certain that her caller was Craig, she sang out her greeting.

"Hell…o… Oh."

"Did you hit the lottery, or is that handsome hunk on his way over? I was gon' bring you some rockfish soon as I finished grilling them. My boss and his buddies were fishing over in the Chesapeake Bay and caught oodles of them. His wife told him to take them back to the Bay, so he brought some to the gang that does the commercials. I guess he thinks us black folk freak out on fish. I didn't care, because the supermarket charges eight dollars a pound for these fish."

"I didn't hit the lottery, and he's not coming over. He's going to call, but I'd planned to do some painting."

"It's only five o'clock. You can paint for an hour or so, and I'll put the rest of the rockfish in my freezer and cook them tomorrow. Tie that guy down. If he was mine, I'd know the inside of his ears. He wouldn't get away from me."

"I'd better get busy, Noreen. Talk with you later."

Quickly, she set up her easel and halogen lamp, drank a glass of tomato juice to stave off hunger, selected a paintbrush and began putting the finishing touches on a moonlit-night landscape. Exasperated and dissatisfied with the painting, she considered throwing it away until she suddenly envisaged a small night animal and her young crossing the road. She added a mother raccoon and her two offspring strolling to the other side of the road.

"Great!" she said aloud. "I may be a painter yet." An ecstatic phone call brought Noreen over to view the painting.

"I tell you, girl, you better do something about this. You're good…at least to my untrained eyes. If I were you, I'd ask Craig Jackson what he thinks. He's put on a couple programs about art."

She hugged Noreen. "That's a good idea. Thanks. I will. I wish I knew where I'm headed with him. He cares a lot for me, but as well as I know him, I don't know hardly anything about him…provided that makes any sense."

"Don't stand for it. Ask him questions and insist that he answer you. If he balks, tell him it's important to you, but don't threaten him."

"Oh, I wouldn't do that." She heard her cell phone's pan flute sound. "Dr. Moran speaking. How may I help you?"

"You can have dinner with me."

Kisha glanced at Noreen with a plea for privacy, and Noreen left the room. "Okay, but I want you to take a minute to look at something, so plan for an extra fifteen minutes. What time will you be here?"

"Seven-thirty. Any place special you'd like to go?"

"No. Whatever you choose is fine with me."

"All right. See you soon. Kisses."

She made the sound of a kiss. "Bye, love."

Noreen walked back into the dining room. "If he's coming over, I'll see you later." She gazed at the painting. "That's lovely. You get that brother on the right track. He's got the courage to tell people what's what night after night, and he can carry himself like a giant stepping over big boulders, so he ought to have the courage to let you see him cry. And I'm not saying anything else on this topic."

Her kiss on the cheek surprised Kisha, for she hadn't thought Noreen a demonstrative person. "Say a few prayers for guidance, honey, and it'll work out just fine."

# Chapter 8

Kisha tried not to seem too excited when she opened the door. She looked at her hands, saw the little patches of paint on her fingers and wondered what else she'd done or hadn't done that would tell him how eager she was to be alone with him. He looked down at her, grinned and kissed her nose.

"Hi, sweetheart. What's that green and red stuff on the side of your nose?"

"On the side of my…" She rubbed her face with the back of her hand. "I must have smeared some paint on my face. Does that mean I don't get a real kiss?"

He laid a bunch of red, yellow, purple and white calla lilies on the table, put his arms around her and gazed down into her face. His eyes darkened. Then she felt his mouth on hers, and his tongue sliding back and forth over the seam of her lips, electrifying her. The tips of her breasts hardened as tremors shot through her, titillating and exciting her. He pulled her tighter to him and dipped into her, testing, savoring and anointing every crevice of her mouth. She heard her moans mingle with his, and tightened her hold on him. She pressed his hand to her aching left nipple, dying for the feel of his moist hot mouth tugging on it.

Craig trapped her between himself and the wall, braced his hands above her head and took long and deep breaths. "If we don't stop this right now, baby, I won't leave here until tomorrow morning, and I won't care whether I eat or not. Kisha, we have to do something about this." She didn't say anything. She couldn't. He'd taken away her breath and her will to do anything but accede to *his* will.

After a while, with his arms once more around her, he blew out a long breath and asked her, "Are you all right? I mean can you show me what you wanted to show me?"

Momentarily, she'd forgotten about the painting. She took his hand, walked with him toward the dining room and stopped short when she saw a reflection of herself in the hall mirror. She slapped her hand over her mouth.

"Oops!"

"What's the matter?"

"Do you see what I'm wearing? Excuse me. I have to get dressed."

"But would you please show me what you wanted me to see."

She walked with him into the dining room and pointed to the painting. "Look at that. I'll be right back."

How could she possibly have forgotten her painter's smock and the paint on her hands? She washed up, put on a red dress, remembered that red was an invitation and exchanged it for a green one. After rubbing her face with a soft towel, she brushed her lips with gloss and sped down the stairs.

Had she invested too much of herself in this man? And why did she seem so eager to slide back into the trap from which she had so mercifully been delivered two short years earlier? Granted that Craig differed in the most important ways from Jonathan, but they had the same penchant for not revealing themselves. And hadn't her mother said that a woman's taste in men doesn't change unless she gets an awful shock.

Well, Jonathan had certainly given her the surprise of her then twenty-eight years, and though it hadn't been easy to get him out of her system, she'd done it and was proud of that fact. A man who would lead a woman to believe he was single when, in fact, he had a wife and was, at best, unprincipled and unscrupulous. She didn't believe that of Craig, but she didn't trust her instincts when it came to men.

She paused at the bottom step. She wondered if she was trying to make Craig pay for Jonathan's misdeed. "There's no comparison," she said to herself, "and I'm not going to behave as if there is." She headed for the dining room and looked up at him, waiting for his verdict.

He stood before the painting, gazing as if enchanted. "That was fast," he said, referring to the pace at which she'd washed up and changed her clothes. "When did you do this? I assume it's the reason for the paint on your face and clothes."

"Painting is my hobby. I was hard at it when you called. What do you think?"

"I think you could make a very good living doing this. You are really good."

"You think so? My neighbor's been after me to have a show, but I don't know if I'm good enough for that."

"Trust me, you are. I'd buy this one if I'd never seen you. How many do you have?"

"Forty or fifty. About half of them are scenes from various places in Florida, although I have urban, mountain and winter scenes, too. I'm mainly a landscape painter."

"You should put together a show in a good gallery. Take three of your best to any reputable gallery here, and I'll bet you have a show."

She stared at him. "Are you serious?"

"Kisha, I wouldn't mislead you about this or any other thing. I've looked at paintings in galleries and museums from the Metropolitan Museum of Art in New York to the Louvre in Paris and the Uffizi in Florence. I know art when I see it."

"Okay. I believe you, and I'll get to work on it tomorrow."

He grasped both of her shoulders and stared into her eyes. "Don't forget to keep me posted. You'll need somebody you trust to lift stuff, and I'll be at your disposal."

She couldn't fully appreciate the value of his advice, but she was happy to be with him on warm and loving terms again, so she stood on tiptoe and hugged him. "You're sweet. Precisely to my taste."

"Don't say such things if you don't mean them."

"You are sweet. Let's go. I'm getting hungry."

"That's a ritzy street," Kisha said to Craig when they crossed Abell Avenue. "I tried to find a house on that street, but nobody was selling, and the real estate agent had the crassness to suggest that if anyone wanted to sell, I probably couldn't afford the price tag."

"Oh, I don't know," he said. "I've lived on that street for the past four years. I don't have a house, but I own a co-op apartment."

She clamped her teeth shut, because anything that rolled out of her mouth would be contentious. Didn't he know that after all the time they'd known each other, she should have been to his home. At the least, she should know his address.

"How's your tooth?" she asked, changing the subject.

"My tooth is fine. I have a wonderful dentist, and whatever she does, she does it thoroughly and to perfection."

He stopped for a red light, and she turned fully to look at him. "Are we still talking about your tooth?"

A frown floated briefly over his countenance. Then, laughter poured out of him, and she suspected that if restless drivers behind them hadn't resorted to honking, Craig might have succumbed to hysteria.

"Yeah," he said, "but that would cover other things I know about you, as well." He parked in front of a restaurant famed for its pulled pork barbecue and hot peach cobbler. "This is my first choice, but if you'd like something lighter or more elegant…"

"You know how I love this barbecue. Thanks for choosing it," she said.

After a meal that she thought was as close to soul food as barbecue could be, they stepped outside the restaurant into the biting cold. "Just look at that moon," Craig said. "Not a star or a cloud in the sky. It's a beautiful sight. When I was little," he went on, almost as if he were speaking to himself, "I'd sit in our garden on summer nights and travel all over the world with the moon as my guide. At one time, I wanted to be an astronomer. The moon and stars fascinated me. When I was twelve, I got a powerful telescope for Christmas. How I loved that thing! Looking back, I wonder how my folks got me to put it down long enough to eat. I was enchanted with celestial phenomena."

She wasn't going to remark on his having shared that

bit of himself with her, because she wanted to avoid the appearance of criticizing him. She let him help her into his car. "The more I learn about you, the more interesting you are," she said when he got into the car. "You know, I always wanted to paint, but I never figured I'd be able to make a living at it, and I was good in sciences, so I went for dentistry. I don't have the stomach for medicine and what doctors have to go through during internship. I'm happy with my choice."

"And so you should be. You're the best dentist I ever had as well as the most comforting. When will you start looking for a gallery?"

"Tomorrow morning."

Almost at once, she found an opening at the Penn Gallery. Mitchell Penn, the gallery owner, encouraged her to put the show on immediately. After dinner the next evening, she told Craig of her plans.

"Don't worry. I'll help you with it. Let's plan a reception with little sandwiches, cheese, fruit and wine. I know a good caterer. He'll supply everything, including a bartender."

"But won't that be expensive?"

"No. He's a good friend and a frat buddy. Owns a string of restaurants and fitness clubs. His bill will only reflect the costs. Leave it to me. I encouraged you to do this, and you can count on me." He parked in front of her house and turned to her. "In this and in all things, Kisha, I'll always be here for you."

"Thanks…on condition that you give me the bill for the reception. I need you to care for me, Craig, but I need my dignity, too." She believed he'd be there for her, but would he share with her that part of himself that he guarded so carefully, and did he know how much he told her when he reminisced about his dreams of being an astronomer. Why hadn't he pursued that dream, she wondered.

"I want to kiss you good-night," he said.

A giggle escaped her and, as hard as she tried, she couldn't control that evidence of her amusement.

"What's funny?"

"You're always the one who puts on the brakes," she reminded him.

He planted a short, chaste kiss on her lips. She didn't mind the brevity of his kiss, because she was back in his arms where she belonged.

He stopped kissing and stared at her. "What kind of message are you sending me?"

"None. Just marking my spot. You be sure it stays empty till I get back there."

"And you do the same," he said without the hint of a smile. "I don't want another man's hands near you. Do you understand me?"

"Are you saying we shouldn't see other people?"

He didn't give quarter. "That's precisely what I'm saying. We went over this once before. I'm serious."

"Me, too. Get home safely," she said and watched him drive away.

Craig awoke the next morning an hour earlier than usual, got the pad and pen that he kept on his night table and jotted down the things he had to do that day. He cut short his shower—usually a pleasant twenty-minute routine—splashed half a cup of instant coffee down his throat and headed for Washington, D.C. Forty minutes later, he knocked on Jerry Osborne's apartment door.

"Come in," Jerry said, opening his arms for a bear hug. "I was just about to eat breakfast. What's up?"

"Feed me and pour some good coffee down my throat, and I'll tell you."

"You're on," Jerry said.

The housekeeper put a breakfast of orange juice, cinnamon waffles, strawberries, sausage, whipped cream and coffee in front of them. Craig thanked the woman, then turned to Jerry and told him the reason for his visit.

"How important is this woman to you?"

"Given a choice between her and the Hope Diamond, I wouldn't hesitate. I'd choose her."

"Okay. I'll pull out all the stops."

"She told me she wants the bill, and if I don't give her one, there'll be hell to pay."

"Yeah? I'll keep that in mind when I make out the bill. You got yourself a good woman. Deliver me from female leeches. Since the reception starts at five, I'll be there at three. Tell her not to worry about a thing, not even a toothpick."

"Thanks, Jerry. I owe you one."

"It's nothing, man. You'd do as much for me." They sealed their agreement with a high five and a fist bump, and Craig headed back to Baltimore. He stopped by Penn Gallery for an idea as to how many paintings the gallery could accommodate and went on to his office, where he dialed Kisha's office phone number.

"Dr. Moran's office. How may I help you?"

"This is Craig Jackson. May I speak with Dr. Moran?"

"Just a minute, Mr. Jackson." After a few seconds, the receptionist told him, "She'll call you on your cell phone in five or ten minutes." He thanked her and hung up.

Craig answered a knock on his door, and shock reverberated throughout his system when his boss, Milt Sardon walked in. If Sardon wanted to talk with an employee, he sent for the person. He never went to an employee's office.

Gathering his wits and manners as quickly as he could, Craig stood. "Good morning, Milt. What can I do for you?"

"Take a seat, Craig," Milt said and sat in the chair beside Craig's desk. "Your program on immigrants was a record breaker, and the folks in New York want you to do a weekly show, a roving reporter, something like "Our Man in Las Vegas" or Rome or Copenhagen or any other really interesting place you want to spend a week in. They want my recommendation. I hate to lose you from my six o'clock staff, but I'll do what's right and give the bosses the green light on the condition that you'll broadcast your show from this station."

Craig leaned back, took a deep breath and closed his eyes. His time had come. He was going to have a network program, and he hadn't had to ask for it. He looked at Milt, who seemed to be on edge waiting for his answer, winked and extended his hand.

"Thanks, Milt. That's blackmail I can live with."

Milt stared at him for a minute and then shook with laughter. "You're right, Craig. I hadn't thought of it as blackmail. Your last newscast will be on Thursday evening. On Friday morning, clean out your desk and pack whatever you want to take to your new office. You'll have a nice thick carpet on the floor and draperies at the windows. Myrna will bring you some samples this afternoon, and you can choose your colors. You've done extremely well, man. Leave the last two minutes of your Thursday evening program for me." They shook hands, and Milt Sardon walked out, leaving Craig dumbfounded. The ringing phone brought him out of his mental meanderings.

"Jackson speaking."

"Hi. Sorry, but I was in the middle of a molar when you called."

He had to laugh at that. "How are you, sweetheart. I called to tell you that it's all set for the reception. Jerry Osborne's the man. We had breakfast at his home this morning, and he said he'll be there at three o'clock with everything. You can depend on it."

"That's great. Thanks so much."

"We need some fliers, and let's run over to the gallery on lunch hour and see if Penn won't send out invitations to his customers."

"Okay, and I have to choose twenty-five of my best paintings and… Oh, honey, I'm getting so nervous. Suppose nobody comes."

"The place will be crowded. Trust me." And he'd see to that. He planned to plug the opening at the end of his newscast.

He and Kisha went to the gallery at lunchtime as planned, and he tried to envisage the show, but couldn't because he'd seen only one of her paintings. "She's a terrific artist, fresh and different," Penn said. "I think her work will sell well, and I'm happy that she came to me." He agreed to send out the invitations. "I'll send you fifty or so for your friends and family," he said.

"I wish I knew fifty people I could call friend," Kisha said to Craig later. They'd spent too much time at the gallery and didn't have time for lunch in a restaurant. Craig bought two orders of barbecued chicken wings, biscuits and coffee and gave one to Kisha.

"They're supposed to be finger-licking good," he said. "I'll call you this evening." He wanted to see her after he left the station, but she needed to choose paintings for her show and, anyway, he meant to practice self-control. His father liked to say that familiarity bred contempt, and he didn't want to learn the veracity of that proverb from personal experience.

He went back to work and telephoned his father. "I got some good news today, and it means that I'm not likely to join you in the practice of law."

"What? Well, I've kind of expected that. Congratulations. What will you be doing and where?"

He told him about his conversation with Milt Sardon. "Dad, I wouldn't have dared ask for a plum like that. I'm still flabbergasted."

"You'll do well, son. I can't begin to tell you how proud I am. Your mother will be ecstatic."

"I'll call her tonight. Gotta go."

He hung up, and his thoughts went to Kisha. *Kisha!* He hadn't thought to tell her about the prize he'd been given. Understanding began to dawn on him. *So that's what she meant. Something so important to me, the fruition of my dreams, and I spent an hour and a half with her and didn't think to tell her.* He dialed her number.

"Kisha, I have something to tell you," he said without preliminaries, almost as if he had something to fear and was anxious to get it out.

"What? What is it?" she asked, and he could feel her anxiety.

"It's all good. I'll be leaving the six o'clock news at the end of this week. I've been given my own network program."

"Oh, my goodness. You frightened me. This is wonder-

ful. Craig, I'm so happy for you. And I'm terribly proud
of you. Will you have to move to New York?"

"No. Thank goodness. This will remain my home
station. Look, I had to tell you. It's what I've worked for,
and I'm feeling good right now. Tell you more later."

*There. That wasn't so hard, was it?* a niggling voice
said. Strange. He wanted his father to be proud of him,
but he realized that he valued Kisha's respect and pride
in him even more.

On the Friday night before her Saturday show, Kisha
and Craig sorted the paintings, cataloged them and, with
Penn's help, decided how to hang them. When they left
the gallery around midnight, Kisha could finally believe
that she was indeed going to have a showing of her paintings.

"It's going to be a huge success," Craig assured her as
they sat in an all night White Castle restaurant consuming
sliders, fries and coffee.

She wished she could be as certain. "Do you really think
so? I wish my parents were alive to see this. My mother
always believed I had talent as a artist. I've never been con-
vinced, I only knew that I was driven to paint."

"Your mother was right. We'd better go, because
tomorrow's going to be a very long day." He pressed his
lips quickly to hers, and she used good sense and let him
get away with that.

"Wear something exotic tomorrow. People think
painters are bohemians."

Laughter rolled out of her. "I'll do exactly that. See you
at noon tomorrow."

She closed the door, watched him drive off and shook her

head in wonder. Craig Jackson was not used to physical work, but he'd worked like a laborer for hours, relieving her of the burden of packing and unpacking the paintings. After moving them around in the gallery several times, he had hung every one of the twenty-six paintings. If she lifted ten pounds, he rushed to relieve her of the burden. And he would be with her tomorrow from the time the gallery door opened until it closed at the end of the reception. It meant something, and that something was not a casual thing. He was telling her that he was there for her. The knowledge gave her a warm feeling of contentment and, she had to admit, a sense of security.

Mindful of Craig's parting advice, the next morning, Kisha was at the nearest drugstore minutes after it opened. She purchased makeup—because she didn't normally wear any—and big, gold-colored hoop earrings. She spent the next hour trying out different looks with the makeup. Satisfied that she could make herself into a bohemian or, at best, Hollywood's idea of a gypsy, she chose a pair of wide-leg black pants and a red velvet tunic. She combed her hair down, folded a red, silk-chiffon scarf and tied it around her head with one end of it hanging below her shoulders. Then, she hung around her neck all of the gold toned, pearl and mock jewel necklaces she'd kept from her college days, added generous dabs of perfume in strategic places, threw a woolen stole across her arm and considered herself dressed for a painter's public.

When her doorbell rang at eleven-thirty, she rushed to open it and, forgetting that she wore makeup in addition to her peculiar costume, Craig's drop-jawed greeting and sharp whistle took her aback.

"What is it? Is something wrong?" she asked him.

"Uh, no. I…uh…I guess I just didn't recognize you."

"You told me to wear something exotic. I wouldn't look exotic without makeup, would I?"

"Trust me, baby. I am definitely not complaining. It wouldn't be possible to make you anything other than gorgeous. But, sweetheart, this is one hell of a metamorphosis." He twisted his face into a frown.

"Let's go."

He draped the stole around her shoulders, hugged her and propelled her out of the door. They reached the gallery in record time, at least it seemed that way to Kisha.

"Shouldn't we eat something?"

"I'm too nervous to eat," she replied.

"I'm going to Frank's and get us a couple of sandwiches and some coffee."

She didn't object. He was batting a thousand with her, and she saw no reason to oppose him. She strolled around the gallery looking at her work and had to push back the tears of joy. She'd never felt so good about anything.

Craig returned with their food, and they ate it sitting in Penn's office. "I didn't realize it, but I was hungry," she said.

He stopped eating and looked at her. "If you give me a chance, Kisha, I'll always take care of you."

The love she saw in his eyes sent frissons of heat skittering through her. She reached toward him, and he grasped her hand. "Don't think for a moment that I'll let you slide inconsequentially out of my life, Kisha. If I lose you, it won't be for lack of effort on my part," he said.

"Why would you choose a time like this to say such things to me? I'm so strung out, that my response to you may not do either of us justice," she said. Then she patted his hand. "Believe me, I'm not anxious for you to walk out of my life."

A grin started around his bottom lip and drifted over his face until his eyes sparkled and his white teeth flashed. The backs of his long fingers brushed her cheek so softly that she barely felt it. She kissed their tips as he moved his hand from her face. "At least you're on the same page with me," he said.

The caterer arrived at three o'clock as promised bringing with him a curved bar, three microwave ovens, a bartender and five uniformed waiters. "I have enough food and drink for two hundred," Jerry told Kisha.

"Two hundred what?"

"You'll see. This place will be crowded."

And so it was. At about five-thirty, the mayor arrived and shortly thereafter a camera crew and reporter from WWRM-TV, the station for which Craig worked, greeted her as if she were an old friend. "I'm glad to meet you, Dr. Moran. Craig told me your stuff is fabulous. Can you answer a couple of questions? I want to get this on the eleven o'clock news." She answered the questions and thanked the reporter for coming.

"I've had a lot of openings," Penn told her, "but I've never had a shindig like this. Man, this is over-the-top. Already over two hundred people walked in here. I quit counting."

"Any sales?" she asked him.

"Oh, yeah. Five, and we've just started."

Kisha tried to focus on her surroundings, but she felt as if she were in a dream. Guests hung around Craig, greeting him and asking for his autograph. She remembered that he'd changed jobs, but she hadn't caught his last program or any of his recent programs, for that matter. But he never left her for more than a minute. He would always return, drape his arm around her, introduce her to someone, show in little ways that she was special to him.

"I never dreamed we'd have a full house," she said to Penn when he came to tell her he'd sold a small painting of a robin with a squirrel in a spring garden.

"It had some terrific advertising. I expected the people would turn out, and they're definitely getting a first-class reception."

When nine o'clock arrived, fourteen of the twenty-six paintings, including the three most expensive had been sold, and she was ready to pass out. "You may leave the remaining paintings here," Penn told her, "and I'll have at least four of them hung all the time." He looked straight at her. "That is, if you'll give me an exclusive." She agreed, asked Jerry for the bill and looked around for Craig.

"I'll mail it to you," Jerry told her. "You put on a great show. Call me anytime you need a caterer."

"I'm dying to kick off my shoes," she told Craig as they walked up the driveway to her house. "I feel as good as I did the day the dean gave me my DMD diploma. This was a dream come true. I don't know how to thank you."

"Don't thank me, Kisha. When you're happy, so am I."

"Want to come in?" she asked him. He said nothing, opened the door with her key, handed her the key, closed the door behind them. She looked at him with what she knew was an expression of puzzlement. She couldn't read his somber expression.

"Have a seat while I scrub this stuff off my face," she said.

He took out his handkerchief and handed it to her. "You can take off the lipstick, but please leave the rest. Right now, I want the woman that that costume represents. Carefree, wild and adventurous."

"Is that the way I look?"

"Yeah, and it suits you...at least for today." Without

warning, he buried his face in the curve of her neck. She grasped him to her and felt him tremble. She shed her fatigue as quickly as wind-driven leaves fall from trees in late autumn.

"I'm so proud of you, Kisha. I wanted all those people to know that you belong to me."

"I'm sure they guessed," she said stroking his back. "Would you like some coffee?"

"I don't need any coffee. I need *you*."

Implicit in his simple words was a promise of fulfillment. She knew what it meant to be in his arms with him buried deep inside of her. He smelled of cologne, of power and of man, and she was caught up in his aura like a bug in a spider's web. But she didn't want to extricate herself. She wanted to dive deeper into his lover's lair. She guided his mouth to her parted lips and took him in. His hands traveled over her back and shoulders, rubbing, searching, possessing. She sucked vigorously on his tongue, but it wasn't enough.

"I want to feel your mouth on me."

"Tell me what you want. I want to please you. Tell me," he urged.

"Take this thing off me. I want to feel my nipple in your mouth." She threw back her head. "I love the way that feels."

He unzipped her tunic and as it fell to the floor, he bent his head to the breast that she held to his lips. "Oh! Ohhhhh." She cried as he sucked it into his warm mouth. With both hands, he gripped her buttocks to him and let her feel him bulge against her. When she began to undulate wildly, he picked her up and took her up the stairs to her bed. Within seconds he had her on her bed, nude except for her bikini panties and was stripping himself as fast as he could.

He put one knee on the bed, looked down at her and smiled the sweetest smile she'd ever seen. She couldn't get him to her fast enough, and with her arms wide and her legs spread out she welcomed him. He tumbled into her arms, and she locked him to her. He began to feather kisses over her eyes, nose, cheeks and lips, but she needed it hard and fast. She attempted to pull him on to her and take it the way she needed it.

"You're not ready, sweetheart," he said and kissed his way down her body. She held her breath till he kissed the inside of her thighs, moved back up and teased her with the tip of his tongue.

"I want you in me. Get in me. Craig, stop teasing me."

She felt his tongue caress into her and let out a keening cry, but he pulled away, let his talented fingers play their tune with the skill of a harpist plucking the strings until she moaned for relief.

He moved up her body, slowly, kissing every part of her that he could reach. "Take me in, sweetheart. He sucked her nipple into his mouth and began to suckle her feverishly as if he were starved. She drew her legs up, took his penis into her hands, stroked if lovingly and brought it to her vagina. He tightened his buttocks and went into her. She didn't try to stifle her cries of pleasure as he drove into her, taking her to the edge, bringing her back and taking her there again. He knew her body, and played it to perfection. Out of her mind with desire, she wrapped her ankles over his thighs and rocked with him, grinding her hips up to him in wild undulations.

"Baby, watch it. You'll make me lose it."

She didn't care. The throbbing and squeezing in her vagina had become unbearable. She wanted to burst.

"Be still, baby," he said, unleashed a torrent of power and drove her to climax. Screams poured out of her, and then she collapsed.

"Oh, Craig. Craig. I love you so." His tremors shook her as he shouted his release.

"You're everything to me. *Everything!* Oh, sweetheart, I love you."

*She wanted to believe him. She also wanted to believe herself. Did they love each other? How was she to know?*

# Chapter 9

Kisha sat up in bed, fighting back the tears. She was damned if she'd cry. All she wanted was to feel as if nothing separated her from Craig, and she'd almost driven herself into a frenzy groping for that moment when she wouldn't know the difference between herself and him. She'd almost made it, and then it slipped away. But she wouldn't give up, she couldn't. He said he loved her, but she'd been told that at such a moment, a man was liable to say anything.

She grabbed the pillow and sniffed the place where his head had lain, taking in a whiff of his cologne. Then, she rolled over into the musky odor of his body and the scent of their loving. She pounded the pillow in frustration, climbed out of bed and trod down the stairs to put the chain on the door.

*Something has to give, and I hope it won't be me.*

* * *

After staring at the ceiling for hours, Craig got out of bed, got a bottle of beer from the refrigerator, turned the heat up in his den and sat down. She'd given herself to him in a wild, almost desperate frenzy. He couldn't ask a woman for more. She'd anticipated his needs and his moves even as she made her own demands. And why?

He was not trying to buy her affection. God help him if he was wrong. A long, heavy sigh escaped him. For all that, she'd made love with him until he was no longer himself, and she could have done with him whatever she wanted. He drained the bottle and suppressed a desire to throw it as far as his strength would allow. He must be wrong. He had to be. He'd swear by Kisha Moran's integrity.

Still, the thought wouldn't leave him. He didn't care less for her, but when he called her later that morning it was out of duty and concern for her feelings. "How are you this morning?" he asked after she greeted him. He knew he sounded formal, but pretense was not his strong point.

"I don't know," she said. Apparently she wasn't good at pretending, either.

"What's the matter?"

"Same old. Same old. Last night, I tried so hard to…to reach you, to feel that…I don't know… Maybe the problem is me, and I'm looking for something that doesn't exist, but I'd give anything if just once I could feel that nothing separated me from you."

"From the way you responded to me, one would have thought that you got all you wanted and needed. Look, Kisha, this is a bit heavy for me right now. I'll check back with you." But he didn't and as hard as he tried to call her and patch it up, he couldn't make himself do it. He supposed they'd get over that hump, and he prayed that they would, but he meant to give her time to look inward and find her role in the breach of their relationship.

He told his superiors at the network that he did not care to spend Christmas in Florence, Italy, and that he intended to enjoy the holidays with loved ones. In his mind's eye, he saw Kisha sitting with him and his parents before a fire in his parents' great stone fireplace. He pictured her helping them hang bells and other trinkets on the huge Christmas tree that he knew his father would place near the fireplace.

"She's deep inside of me," he said to himself, "and there's nothing I can do, but fix things up between us."

Kisha gazed at the check she received from the Penn Gallery, unable to believe what she saw. She reached for the phone to call Craig, remembered the chill between them and hung up. Several minutes later, the phone rang and, when she answered, she heard Noreen's voice.

"Girl, you won't believe this. I just got my first check. These people must think money grows on trees. Girl, I never made this much in a whole year. I'm gon' send out for some goodies, so come on over. No point in enjoying this by myself."

"Okay. Give me half an hour." Kisha folded the letter, put it in the pocket of her jeans, threw on her shearling coat and went next door to Noreen's house. Her friend greeted her with an enthusiastic embrace.

"Girl, times have changed. I'm not going to be dirt-poor any more." She paused and frowned. "That is, not 'less I bungle this contract. Come on in. We're gonna have

Jamaican meat patties, a salad, cheese cake and white wine. Say, you down about something?"

Kisha flexed her right shoulder in a quick shrug. "Life's kicking me in the butt right now, but as they say, 'this too shall pass.' The gallery sold eleven of my paintings, and I've got a six-figure check here." She pulled the paper out of her jeans pocket and showed it to Noreen.

"You go 'way from here."

"Yes, indeed. And the first figure starts with a two. Can you beat that?"

"You see? And you had all that money just molding away in your basement. Girl, this don't call for wine, this is a scotch and soda occasion."

"Maybe, but I think I'd better stick to wine."

"All right. So what's with tall, dark and drop-dead handsome? He was eating you up yesterday at your show. The brother couldn't keep his hands off you. And child, you should've seen yourself in that outfit. Sex personified."

"It's not working, Noreen."

Noreen put the patties and salad on the table along with a dish of deviled eggs and said the grace. Then, she propped her elbows on the table and regarded Kisha intently.

"Girl, you gon' have to ease up. You told him what you needed, and now, you just gon' have to give him time and space to do it. If a man like that one looked at me the way he looked at you Saturday in front of all those people, I'd manage to lead him where I wanted him to go.

"Talking and demanding things don't get you what you want out of a man. At least, not any man I ever knew. Try a little softness…and some tenderness."

"But Noreen—"

"I know they say if it don't come easy, let it alone, but

if it's not worth a little of your sweat, maybe it's not worth having," Noreen said.

"I got it."

Noreen passed the eggs to Kisha. "I wonder if you do. And don't have no cut-and-dried talks with him about personal…you know, intimate…things like you're sitting in a boardroom dishing it out to a CEO. That is, not unless you're mad at him. By the way, that free advertising he did for you on WWRM-TV must have been worth thousands. You be careful. That man cares a lot for you."

Kisha placed her fork on her plate, carefully and slowly. "What free advertising are you talking about?"

Noreen's left eyebrow shot up. "Don't you watch his nightly news program? Every night for a week, he told the viewers about your show and the free dental care you give to kids. He even said he planned to be at the reception and hoped to meet them there."

"You're not serious," Kisha said, leaning back in her chair and gazing intently at Noreen.

"Would I lie about a thing like that?"

Kisha rubbed her forehead with the fingertips of her right hand. "No. I don't suppose you would."

Returning home, she wrapped her coat tightly around her body against the cold and dampness. For a brief moment, she longed for the warm sunshine of the Florida Keys. Then, she recalled the sheer bliss she'd known in Craig's arms. Baltimore wasn't so bad.

However, when she looked out of her bedroom window the next morning, Monday, and saw at least four feet of show, she resigned herself to remaining at home. The choice was an easy one, she realized, because she couldn't open her front door.

* * *

Craig looked out of his bedroom window at the men blowing and shoveling snow from the sidewalks in front of the building in which he lived. He made up his mind at once, dressed and went to the basement garage, where he borrowed a shovel from the building's superintendent and headed for Kisha's house.

Because only main thoroughfares and streets near schools and hospitals had been cleaned, he had to take a circuitous route. When he saw that Kisha couldn't open her front door, his decision to clean away the snow from her property gave him a feeling of satisfaction. After working for more than two hours, his fingers had become stiff, and his face felt like a sheet of ice, but he meant to finish it.

"Come inside, Craig, and at least warm your hands. You must be freezing."

He looked up, saw her hunched in the doorway as if trying to shield herself from the frigid air. "Thanks, but I'm all right. I'll be done in a few minutes."

"I appreciate your help. I couldn't even open the door. Please come in at least for a few minutes."

If he refused, he'd drive one more nail into the coffin of their relationship. He didn't want a few minutes of hospitality and hot coffee with her. He needed her at her deepest and most honest level. And he needed assurance that when she'd been wild beneath him the night after her show, she wasn't thanking him for his contribution to her success.

She opened the door wider, and he saw that she shivered from the cold. "Please come in, if only for a little while."

He didn't want to hurt her, so he turned off the blower and walked slowly up the steps. She remained standing in the doorway until he reached her. And still, she didn't move. He either had to move her or ask her to let him pass. She gazed up at him, so close that he squeezed his hands into fists to avoid grasping her body.

"Hi. I made fresh coffee and warmed some cinnamon buns. Have some." She took his hand, closed the door and walked with him to the kitchen, where she'd put two place settings on the little table. "I was wondering how I'd get out of this house if I had an emergency."

He'd wondered the same thing. But what he said as he bit into a cinnamon bun was, "You'd have managed." He chewed the bun and she sat with him while he ate. "This is good. Did you make them?" It was an inane question, but he was not going to discuss their relationship in that casual atmosphere. It was not the time for it. Neither of them had made a special effort to straighten out the situation, and that meant neither was ready to do so.

He intended to try one more time, and if they couldn't effect a true meeting of mind and spirit, he'd kiss it goodbye for good. It would hurt, but he'd hurt before, and he knew that although he'd be in for a difficult and painful time, it wouldn't kill him.

"No," she said. "They came out of a package. I only baked them."

He sipped the coffee. "I don't feel like making talk with you, Kisha, and we wouldn't settle anything right now if we talked seriously. Thanks for the coffee. It hit the spot. After I finish cleaning the sidewalk, I'll head home. If you need anything, call me."

One part of him longed to hold her and love her, but another, more rational part, knew that if he did, he'd only make himself more miserable. He needed a resolution of the problem, and he meant to hold out for that.

He finished clearing the snow from around her property, put the plow and shovel into the trunk of his Mercedes and headed home. The pains in his belly told him he should have eaten more that day than a single cinnamon bun.

When Craig arrived at home he decided to outline his first "Our Man In…" project. But he couldn't get excited about his original idea of revisiting the aftermath of the assassination of Martin Luther King, Jr.

He stepped out on his balcony and threw some peanuts to the wild squirrel that he'd sort of adopted. He looked out at the snowflakes drifting down and went back inside. What a perfect day to sit with Kisha in front of the fire in his den. She probably wondered why he hadn't invited her to his home. To him, it would mean that he'd opened the doors of his life to her.

"I'm roasting chestnuts in the fireplace," Noreen said. "I love to smell 'em when it's cold and snowing. Want to come over?"

Kisha was not in the mood for Noreen's or anyone else's company, other than Craig's. "Thanks. You know I love chestnuts, but I'm real busy right now. Another time."

She checked her answering service, and since she didn't have any emergency calls, she decided to remain home and paint for the remainder of the day. Around three o'clock that afternoon, she went to the foyer closet to remove a small date book from the pocket of her jacket and saw a billfold on the floor. She picked it up and called Craig, happy for an excuse to talk with him.

"Jackson speaking."

"Hello, Craig. This is Kisha. Do you have your billfold? I found one on the floor in my foyer. I haven't opened it, but I assume it's yours, because you're the only man who's been here."

"My wallet? Just a minute. It isn't in my pocket. I must have dropped it when I pulled my gloves out of my pocket. I'm glad you called, because I was about to leave to do some shopping. Imagine how embarrassed I would have been."

"I'm glad I found it. Why don't you come by for it. I'm not going out."

"Thanks. I'll be over in about half an hour. Bye for now."

Her first inclination was to freshen up and let her hair down. She started up the stairs and stopped. "I look good enough for me. If he doesn't think I pass muster, tough!" She returned to her painting and was hard at work when he rang the doorbell.

Kisha lifted her chin, brightened her facial expression and opened the door. "Come in."

"I see you're painting. Mind if I have a look at it?"

She led him to the dining room where an easel held her half-done representation of a young girl leaning against a tree beside a lake at sunset.

He stepped close to the painting. "Very idyllic. Is that from memory, or do pictures like this form in your mind and you recreate them on canvas?"

"It popped into my head. I love the water and the woods, and when I lived in the Keys, watching the sunset was one of my greatest pleasures."

He stared at the painting for a long time. "I'd like to buy that one."

There were few things he could have said that would have shocked her more. "Oh, no, Craig. I'd be happy knowing that you have it. I'll give it to you. That you want it will inspire me to hurry and finish it."

"I should have known you'd do that." He turned and looked at her. "Thank you. I'll cherish it."

She could see that he was about to leave, so she fell in step with him as he headed for the door. She hurt, and she didn't care if he knew it. To have his icy treatment without knowing the cause, being with him like two strangers passing in the night…it was too much.

"Here's your billfold." As the words left her lips, her voice broke. He took the billfold from her, and when his fingers touched hers, the electricity from their touch startled both of them.

"Oh!" she said, and if he hadn't grasped her arm, she would have backed away. He loosened his grip, and she jerked away from him, staring into his eyes as she did so. "Craig, please. I've had enough torture today to last me for a lifetime. I can't handle any more."

"Neither can I." His words seemed to tumble out against his will. "Come here. Sweetheart, come here to me." He opened his arms, and she dashed into them, into the haven that she so badly craved.

He clasped her tightly to him, and she soaked up the sweetness and the tenderness of his caress, trembling with a passion that refused to be controlled. She looked up at him, saw the smile on his face, wet her lips and parted them in anticipation of an all-consuming kiss. The gentle pressure of his lips startled her, and in spite of his gentleness, her blood raced to her loins. She tightened her hold on him, moving closer, ready to demand what she wanted. But it was he who orchestrated the exchange.

"I want more, and I need more," he said, in words that were soft and seductive. "But until we resolve all the issues between you and me, nothing else that happens between us will be enough for me. If you're not going out, we'll talk later this evening."

"I'll be at home."

He kissed her quickly, almost as if he was afraid to linger. As he walked down the stairs, Kisha watched his less-than-purposeful strides. Maybe it was that, or could it have been the pain she saw in him as he stood in the foyer looking down at her, pain like the ache in her heart.

He wanted to have dinner with her, to spend the evening enjoying her company, but it would be so easy to return to where they were before they made love last Saturday evening. And he was not going to do that. He wanted them to have a chance at a relationship and, in his view, pushing their problems under the rug was not the way to achieve that. He shrugged. What the hell! Eating dinner alone was not the worst thing that could happen to a man.

At home, he phoned a nearby restaurant, ordered a dinner of broiled lobster, parsleyed potatoes, asparagus and chocolate cheesecake and enjoyed it while sitting in his living room in front of his new flat-screen television set. As he savored the cheesecake, he allowed himself a laugh. In his parents' home, they only ate in the kitchen or the dining room. At his home, he ate wherever he pleased. He took the dishes to the kitchen, put them into the dish-washer, straightened up the kitchen and went back to the living room. After turning off the TV, he kicked off his shoes and dialed Kisha's home phone number.

"Hello, Craig."

Heartened by her warm greeting-so different from the officious style she used when answering her cell phone—

he settled into the soft, leather seat. "Hi, have you looked out your window recently?"

"No. I've been painting, and that means I'm practically in another world."

"That's why your paintings are so interesting. By the way, this coming Thursday night, my first network piece is set to air. It's a study of the people whose houses will be torn down to widen the two turnpikes. I'd rather it hadn't been the first in the series, but my boss said run it now, so now is when it will air.'"

"I didn't realize you'd finished it. Congratulations. Did you learn anything?"

"It doesn't matter how much one person's life is affected, so long as it's for the common good, as the government puts it. Don't those guys in Washington care about the little guy? Some of the situations are tragic."

"And you're not going to edit them out?"

He put his foot on the coffee table. "No way! What I found is what they'll get. Besides, those people need an advocate. Nobody seems to understand that they have rights."

"Isn't there some way to compromise?"

"Yeah. But they don't want to take up those old railroad tracks that haven't been used in half a century. They'd rather destroy ten or fifteen houses."

"Then, there's the conclusion of your story."

His antenna shot up. "What? What did you say?" She repeated it.

"Hold on there. That's perfect. I'll get information on what tearing down those houses will cost, and what it will cost officials to remove those old tracks. I'll bet anything that what I find will help those home owners. Can we talk again tomorrow? I want to get busy on that right now.

Thanks. You can't imagine how much you've helped. I wasn't satisfied with that ending."

"You're welcome. I didn't help all that much, but if you think I did, I'm glad."

"Say, if I screen it, will you come over and take a look? I can still edit the piece, if you find something that I could improve. It won't air for another two weeks, so I can even reinterview if I have to."

"Uh…sure. I'll be glad to. When would you like us to look at it?"

Did she hesitate? Better not put any stock in that. He'd probably surprised her. "Could you come over tomorrow evening? I'll pick you up at home, and then we can stop by this gourmet shop I know, get what we want for dinner and eat at my place. Would that suit you?"

"Fine. I'd like that."

They talked for a few minutes longer, but he was eager to work on the story and he soon said good-night. To his way of thinking, Kisha was a perfect example of why a smart man wouldn't be happy with an airhead. If he listed all the things he liked about Kisha, it would be a while before he got to work on his project.

"I'd better not get into that right now." He started to his office and stopped short. *An hour ago, I was thinking about the consequences of pushing problems under the rug. Yet here I am inviting Kisha here to spend the evening with me eating dinner, drinkin wine and watching my work. And I can't remember when I've been as hungry for a woman as I am now.*

He considered himself to be a strong man, but what he was contemplating seemed more like punishment than temptation. He worked until long after midnight, and he admitted that not since his early days as a journalist had he enjoyed his work as much. He'd reached the level in his field where he no longer did spade-level research, and he missed it, because it was in doing the grunt-work of reporting that he'd learned the fine points of his trade. He fell into bed, exhausted, but happy with what he'd accomplished.

"Now, if I can get things straightened out with Kisha, life will be good. She's the one. If only I can get her to see that, we'd make each other bloom!"

He needn't have worried about that aspect of their relationship, because Kisha had already decided that he made her bloom. She considered the problem as mainly a matter of getting him to understand that and its implications for mutual sharing.

"Hi," she said when she opened the door to him that evening. "I've been looking forward to this evening."

He leaned down and kissed her cheek, and when her eyes widened in surprise, he grasped both of her shoulders. "Do you mind if we straighten out something?" She shook her head to indicate that she didn't.

"I've been in a tizzy all day waiting to see you, and the chances of my behaving sensibly with you tonight aren't good." He raised his hand to prevent her from interrupting him. "I want more for us than gratification, and that's why I kissed you on your cheek. Anything more would be too explosive."

"I see," she said, but he sensed that she didn't.

"We need to talk seriously to dissipate our mutual concerns. So will you spend the weekend with me at my place in Marriottsville? We'll be alone there, and we can speak our minds and our hearts. It's extremely important to me." He released her shoulders and took her hand. "Will you go with me?"

"I want that, too, Craig. It's what's missing in our relationship." She smiled as the expression on his face, that had appeared to be serious concern, dissolved into a grin. "Don't worry, I'll see that you behave. Anytime you need help, just let me know."

"I may regret having told you that. Let's go."

They stopped at a gourmet delicatessen and picked up something to eat, but she hadn't been prepared for the case of nerves that unsettled her as they neared the building in which Craig lived. As they walked into his apartment, she was struck by its apparent spaciousness. The small foyer led to a living room that she guessed to be thirty-five by thirty feet.

She whirled around and looked at him. "This place is huge. But now that I think of it, a small space wouldn't suit you. You're a big guy."

"You're right. I love space. Maybe that's why I'm happy when I'm out of doors."

"Do you play this piano?" she asked as she ran her hand across the Steinway grand.

"Not as often as I'd like. Have a seat, and I'll get our food ready."

She didn't sit down, but walked around looking for telltale signs that would reveal Craig's personality. She found sheet music of Chopin, Gershwin, Joplin, Ellington and Mozart in the piano bench and decided that Craig was a serious pianist. The paintings on the walls were not familiar to her, but they reflected good taste in art. She nearly gasped at the size of his collection of CDs and records.

"You have enough here to open a music store," she said

when he called her to the dining room. "This is a wonderful and tastefully decorated apartment. How many more rooms do you have?"

"Two bedrooms, but I use one of them as my study."

"What do you do about guests?" she asked and immediately wished she hadn't.

"I don't usually have any. I have a couch in my den, and when my parents visit, I sleep there and give them my room."

She changed the subject, because she didn't want him to tell her that any other guest slept with him. "How do you find these wonderful restaurants and food shops?"

"I love good food, and I'll go a long distance in order to get it." When she realized that he wasn't going to say the grace, she said it. He half smiled, and she knew he'd been taught to say grace at meals.

After they ate, she helped him clear the table and straighten up. She was careful not to touch him as they maneuvered around each other in the small kitchen. He had a smile on his face, but she didn't ask him why it was there. She'd learned that she couldn't anticipate the answer she was likely to get from Craig.

He put a bottle of white burgundy wine and two wineglasses on the coffee table, sat beside Kisha on the sofa, put on a DVD and flicked on the television. "I want you to like this, but I'd rather have *your* criticism than complaints from my boss or the critics, so don't be nice."

She knew he didn't want her to trash his work, and she wasn't going to. However, if she could make a useful suggestion, she would. She thought her heart would break at the sight of five little children, all eight and under, she supposed, clinging to their father, who was worried about losing their home.

"Where's their mother?" she asked him at the end of that segment. "The poor man looks as if the weight of the world is on his shoulders."

"She died when the last child was born."

"Could you manage to include that piece of information? A widower with little kids is heartbreaking."

"I'll put that in."

By the end of the one-hour program, she'd had it confirmed that Craig Jackson was as smart as he was eloquent but, more importantly, that he could lock arms with the less fortunate and help them fight their battles.

"It's wonderful, Craig. I'm proud of you. It's meaningful, it can change people's lives for the better and it shows that your superiors judged well when they gave you this opportunity."

She couldn't read the quizzical expression on his face when he said, "You really mean that? You've never told me what you think of my work."

It was her time for puzzlement. "Why, you excel at what you do. I thought you realized that I…that I think your reporting is outstanding."

He seemed to have found something important on his shoes or on the floor around them. She couldn't say which. "No. I didn't realize it, but it's good to know it. Every man wants his woman to have pride in him and in his work."

What was she supposed to say to that? If she said she wasn't his woman, he could rightly consider that a put-down, but on the other hand, she didn't like the idea of being a man's woman. She allowed herself a laugh that caused him to raise an eyebrow.

"What's amusing?"

"Me and my double standards, and please don't ask me to explain that, because I'm not going to."

He narrowed his left eye and showed his glistening teeth in a grin that bloomed all over his face. "So I'm your man, but you're not my woman. Is that it?"

"I refuse to answer on the grounds that—"

"Not to worry. As long as you consider me to be your man, that works for me."

"I want to change the subject."

"Okay. Change it."

"How about playing something for me?"

"I'd be glad to, but I'm warning you, that piano hasn't been tuned in seven months. What else? Your wish is my command."

"I'd like to see the rest of your apartment."

He stood at once and extended his hand. "Come on." He stood at the door of his den, leaning against the wall while she walked around, fingering his notebooks, running her hands over the wood of his bookcases and desk. She looked out of the window.

"My goodness, what a view!" A lake in the park below and the evergreens surrounding it stood out beneath the clear sky and the moon and stars that lighted it. "Doesn't this scene seduce you away from your work."

"We're not going to talk about what seduces me from my work," he said, and when she glanced at him, there was no smile on his face. "When I have work to do, I close the blinds on that scene and on a lot of other temptations. Everything in its own time and place."

She turned back to the window. "I also operate on that principle," she said and prepared to leave. Their conversation was headed toward intimacy, and that was off the docket for the night. "I'd better be going, Craig. I know you're eager to turn in your project. You've done a wonderful job."

"Thanks." He took her hand and walked to the closet at the entrance. He helped her into her coat and kissed her lips. "I had to do that. Thanks for coming and for helping me. I think we make a great team, don't you?"

"Yes, I do." She hadn't meant to sound grudging, but his words had surprised her. She squeezed his hand as they reached his car. "Whenever you think I can help, let me know."

"I take that seriously, Kisha, and I will. Yes, I definitely will."

# Chapter 10

Craig had promised himself that he would try to be more open with Kisha, because that seemed to be very important to her. And when he thought about it, he understood that his comfortable feeling about her and what she meant to him derived in part from his knowledge of her. He knew far more about her than he had allowed her to know about him. Unless she had spent a lot of time doing research on him, and he doubted that, she didn't know enough about him to make a decision about their future.

He started to make notes on what he wanted to include in the DVD as an accommodation to Kisha's suggestion, saw the telephone sitting on his desk and phoned her.

"Hi. This is Craig."

"Hi. Why do you think I don't recognize your voice? I'll bet ninety percent of Baltimore's population recognizes it."

"Point taken. I expect I'd be put out if you said, 'Who's

this?' when I call you. Look, I don't remember telling you
about this, but I'm sponsoring the music education of some
junior high school and high school students. On Thursday
evening they're giving recitals, and I should be there. Will
you go with me?"

"Absolutely. I'll be delighted, and I…I really appreciate your asking me. How wonderful. I'm dying to ask
you a slew of questions about it, but I know you want to
work on that project, so I'll save my questions for later.
What time?"

"The program's at seven. If you can go directly from
your office, we could have an early dinner."

"I can do that. Is five o'clock all right?"

"That's perfect. See you then, and don't forget that
we're leaving Friday afternoon for Marriottsville."

"How could I forget that? What do you wear when
you're there?"

"I take warm things for hiking, fishing, splitting wood
and just knocking around, and ordinary things for indoors.
I built the house and I hope you'll like it."

"If it's half as tasteful as your apartment, I'll love it.
Good night, hon."

"Good night, sweetheart."

He found the telephone number of the second man
he'd interviewed for the project and let out a long sigh of
relief. He could make the changes without returning to
Pennsylvania.

The next morning, he phoned Herbert Bailey, the
widower and single father in his story, with the man's permission, hooked up his tape recorder. Within less than half
an hour, he had the information that he needed. Engineers
at the TV station dubbed it on to the DVD, and he had a copy

for Kisha when he went to meet her. She wanted to know
how he managed to make the revision in such a short time.

He told her about his call to Herbert Bailey. "When I make
up my mind about a thing, I don't waste time doing it."

She looked at him, nodding her head as if in approval,
but he knew that the movement of her head signified understanding, that she had received another small piece to the
puzzle that he represented to her.

After dinner, he drove out Martin Luther King, Jr. Boule-
vard and paused at the corner of McCulloh Street. "This is
the home of the Arena Players. It is the oldest continually
operating African-American theater company in the United
States. They put on plays from September to June. And if
you haven't yet been to the Great Blacks In Wax Museum,
we'll go sometime. It's on East North Avenue at around
Bond Street, and it's really worth the visit."

"I'd love to go. Life in the Florida Keys revolved around
water, sunshine and storms. Culture wasn't high on the list
of things to appreciate."

"I guess not, but it would be good if some of these kids
could get away from the inner city for a week or two."

"Maybe we could get a group of celebrities to sponsor a
program for city children. I mean what does Joe Jack do with
ten or fifteen million a year. He won't miss fifty thousand."

"You're right. but the more money people get, the more
they want." He slowed the car. "There's a parking spot."

They entered by the side entrance of what had once
been a movie theater. "You're in good time, Mr. Jackson,"
a woman of considerable age said. "The children have
been fidgeting all over the place."

He introduced Kisha to Ann Jessup, who guided them to
a front row seat. It pleased him to see that the auditorium

was nearly three-quarters full. After four piano pieces, two guitar recitals, two on violin and one performance on cello, he leaned back for a second and closed his eyes. He'd been told that he wasted his money, but those starry-eyed girls and boys proved him right. Two conductors and one assistant conductor of major symphony orchestras handed him their written comments, and each said that all of the performers deserved scholarships to a reputable music conservatory.

"We'll get scholarships for them," Ann Jessup assured him. "I'm so proud of them."

"What's her connection to this program?" Kisha asked him.

"She's like a house mother. They practice downstairs, because they don't have privacy at home, and she sees that they have food and other things that they need. They get lessons here on Wednesday afternoon and Saturday morning."

"I wonder how much it costs to rent a building like this one."

"It was cheaper to buy it." He'd shocked her, but before the weekend was over, he'd give her more of the same. After congratulating the children and introducing them to Kisha, he put an arm around her shoulder and headed for his car.

She didn't have the temerity to ask him if he owned that building. Maybe he'd gotten a philanthropist to purchase it for his project. Who knew? Noreen had told her that he supported some children's music education, but she hadn't dreamed that the project was such a high-level one. Those children had had very competent teachers who commanded high fees.

"What do you think of the students?"

"I don't know nearly as much about music as you do and as I would like, but I know what pleases my ear and to me, all of them sounded like professionals."

"They have good teachers, and I chose them because they clearly had a natural aptitude for music. You can't imagine how happy I am about their progress."

"I would be, too, Craig, if I had helped those kids realize their dream."

He held her hand as they strolled up the walk to her house. She looked at the perfectly laid concrete shapes on which they walked. Not one thing out of place, and when she got inside her house, she'd find the same. Order and neatness described her life in every way except what, in the long run, probably mattered most. Most any adult would describe her personal life as unacceptable.

"You're doing as much and more when you give an evening each week of free care to children whose parents can't afford to pay for the care of their teeth." He pinched her nose. "Don't forget that. Thanks for coming with me tonight. I've been alone so much for so long that I'm surprised at the pleasure I get from sharing something that's meaningful to me with…with a woman who's important to me."

With his arms around her, he pressed his lips to hers, but when she thought he'd suck her into a whirlpool of passion, he hugged her and released her.

"I'll be here Friday at four." A rueful smile flashed across his face. "Don't ask me how I'll manage to wait till then. Good night."

She didn't want him to leave her, but she knew that indicating that wouldn't be wise. So she kissed his cheek, opened her door and watched him stride away from her. "One of these days I'll stay with him always," she said aloud, "even if I have to sit him down and teach him how to share himself with me. No way am I giving up on that man."

At a few minutes before four o'clock that Friday afternoon, she put her weekend bag beside the door, attempted to sit down in the living room and wait, but jumped up immediately and removed a bit of dust from a lamp shade. Certain that she heard a peculiar noise in the kitchen, she rushed there, but saw nothing amiss. The doorbell rang and, for a moment, she stood frozen in her tracks. Recovering her presence of mind she ran to the door, flung it open and was met with only a gust of cold air. She closed the door, certain that the bell had rung. Realizing that she wasn't wearing perfume, she rushed upstairs to get some and, immediately after she reached her bedroom, the doorbell rang. To satisfy herself that her mind was not deserting her, she looked out of her bedroom window, saw the silver-gray Mercedes in front of the house and raced down the stairs without applying the perfume.

She flung the door wide, saw him standing there and smiled in relief. "What's the matter? I thought you were expecting me," he said before lifting her into his arms and hugging her.

"I was, but I'm not in the habit of spending a weekend with a man."

His right eyebrow shot up. "And what does that mean?" he asked and picked up her bag.

"It means that just because I have a DMD doesn't mean that I have an advanced degree in romance."

"Is that your title? What does it mean?"

"Doctor of Dental Medicine, meaning I did an internship and a hospital residency. I'm a doctor."

"I had no idea. That's wonderful. My hat's off to you and

to any other person who can do that. A residency is tough. You can go for days without an uninterrupted night's sleep."

"Days? You mean weeks, but it was worth it." She locked the door behind them and they settled into his car. "How long is the trip?"

"If the traffic is light, twenty-five minutes, but I want to make a short stop on the way. We need matches, chestnuts and kindling."

"When were you last out there?" she asked him.

"Yesterday afternoon. I wanted everything to be right for your visit, and I leave nothing to chance."

"Thank you. You're such a sweet man."

"You think I'm sweet?" he asked with an echo of surprise in his voice.

"Yeah. I think so. Don't you?"

She loved to hear him laugh, and he treated her to a good dose of it. "Think I'm sweet? If you think so, that's all I need." He stopped at a roadside market a few miles from his house and purchased the items he'd mentioned.

"And to think I almost nixed you, because I thought you'd be full of yourself."

He stopped. "How long did it take you to disabuse yourself of *that* notion?"

She couldn't help laughing at his deadly serious expression. "Not long. By the time you were ready to leave my office the day we met, I'd just about made up my mind to pursue you."

In the darkness of that mid-December late afternoon, she couldn't get a sense of her surroundings when Craig drove into a wooded area and parked in front of a house that seemed at home among the huge old trees.

"We're here," he said in a prideful voice. Lights flicked on at the front door and, taking her arm in a possessive manner, he walked with her to the door of the modern, brown brick structure whose first-floor windows proclaimed cathedral ceilings.

"This is majestic, and so quiet. Do you ever get lonely here?"

His frown told her that she may have asked the wrong question. "Occasionally. Why? Would you be lonely here?"

"Only if I didn't have anyone to enjoy it with."

"You could easily fix that. Piece of cake," he said, opening the door. "But hey, I'm ahead of myself. I came close to carrying you across the threshold. Was that inclination telling me something?"

She gazed into his solemn face. "If you'd done that, you would definitely have told *me* something." She changed the subject. "Craig, this house is beautiful," she said when he flicked on lights that revealed the high ceilings, exquisite carpets and modern furniture. "And we like to live with the same autumn colors."

"Yeah. I already noticed that. Being in your house is like being in an extension of mine. Come. I'll take you to your room. It's a steep climb, so we can take the elevator if you like."

"Thanks, but I'd like to walk up. With all these steps, I don't suppose I can expect to get the treatment Rhett gave Scarlett when he whisked her up those stairs at Tara." She put a longing tone in her voice.

Craig rested her bag on the step, pushed back his topcoat and shoved his hands in the pockets of his trousers. "If you want me to carry you up these stairs, all you have to do is ask. If they were twice as high it wouldn't matter, you're more than worth it." He picked up her bag and continued up the stairs.

"A couple of smart retorts come to mind, but I think I won't go there."

His eyes sparkled, and a grin played around his mouth. She wet her lips with the tip of her tongue, remembered where she was and why and sobered. "Oh, don't let me stop you. You're my guest, and your wish is my command. You can take the elevator up, you can walk up or I can take you in my arms and carry you up. Whatever floats your boat."

He put her bag in a room that was neither masculine nor feminine. A queen-size bed rested on a red carpet, and its covering, the walls and draperies were of a yellow-green or avocado color. She liked it. "This is lovely," she said. "Thank you. Where is your room?"

"I'll be right across the hall, so if you get lonely, just yell."

"Thanks. I'll remember that."

"Come downstairs after you get settled in. I'm going to build a fire and get us some drinks."

She unpacked, changed into a pair of black, natural-waistline gabardine pants and a red V-neck cashmere sweater, combed out her hair, slipped on a pair of Keds and went down the stairs. "Hey, I didn't see that grand," she said aloud, marveling that a man would have two Steinway grands.

"Won't you soil your trousers?" she asked, seeing him on his knees before the fireplace.

"I probably should have changed but, in the winter, this is always the first thing I do when I walk into this house. If some of those sparks landed on me, I'd be out a suit." Apparently satisfied, he stood, looked at her with an expression she couldn't fathom and shook his head as if bemused. "I… Can I just hug you so we can get over this awkwardness? Having you here in my house, I... Sweetheart—"

She reached up, looped her arms around his neck and parted her lips. He went into her, and she told herself to take it easy, but she couldn't. She sucked his tongue into her mouth and held his head for her pleasure as waves of heat sped through her body and headed straight to her vagina. Suddenly, he stepped back.

"Baby, you're like a lighted match on dry grass. I'm starved for you, but I don't want to risk jeopardizing what we both hope will come out of this weekend."

"I know, but...that seems to be the way I respond to you."

A grin altered the contours of his face. "Yeah, and I love it."

He bounded up the stairs, changed into a plaid shirt, jeans and a sweater and took the elevator down, because it was one of the things he enjoyed using in his house. "What do you want to drink?" he asked her when he found her peering out the dining-room window.

"I think you once suggested that I try gin or vodka and tonic on lots of ice. Well, I can do that."

"Take a seat in the living room. I'll be there in a couple of minutes." He brought her drink, scotch and soda for himself, two bowls, a knife, a bag of chestnuts and a cutting board, pulled two Moroccan poufs before the fire and beckoned to her to sit. "If it gets too hot, we'll move back, but it's usually comfortable here." He cut the chestnuts and put them beside the hot coals. "I suggest we eat breakfast at about seven, dress warmly and hike along the Patapsco. We can fish if you'd like."

"Who's going to clean the fish?"

"I'll clean them out by the deck." He shelled a hot chestnut, and handed it to her. "For dinner tonight, we can have deviled shrimp, rice, asparagus and a salad. Or we can have filet mignon and baked potato instead of shrimp and rice. Which would you like?"

"Since you mentioned the shrimp first, I'll have that."

He looked at his watch. "Good. You have seventeen minutes and a half in which to change your mind." He shelled another hot chestnut and handed it to her.

"Thanks, but aren't those shells burning your fingers?"

"I don't want you to burn yours, and I want us to enjoy them while they're hot."

She didn't dare look at him. If she did, she'd start what she knew would end in her bed or his. She stood, pushed her pouf as close to his as she could get it, sat down and leaned her head on his shoulder. The knife fell to the floor, and his arms went around her.

"You can't possibly be an only child," she said, "you're too considerate." Then she seemed to shrivel, but he knew that she feared having created a distance between them by invading his privacy. Yet, she had actually created the opening that he sought in order to begin their healing process.

"But I am. However, my parents didn't spoil me. I had a small weekly allowance, but I had to account for every penny. I had everything I needed and most of what I wanted, but they held me to what I now see was a high standard. We had a…a housekeeper, but I had to keep my room neat."

"Why did you have a housekeeper? Did your mother work?"

"My mother is a pediatrician. Her name is Avery. She has a large practice, but when I was little, she dropped me off at school and got home half an hour after I did. As my dad says, 'She takes no tea for the fever.' She won't let my dad and me smother her with protectiveness. She's very professional, and she can hold her own, but she's soft and sweet."

"I'm glad to know that you love your mother."

"You bet I do. She's always there for me, and I'm there for her." Here comes the hard part, he thought, bracing himself mentally.

"Thank you for telling me about her. Are you close to your father?"

"Yes indeed. My dad is an attorney, a well-known and very successful one, and his dream had been for me to join his law firm, Jackson & Jackson."

She sat up straight. "You? In a law firm?"

"Right. I got a degree in journalism and later I got a law degree at Harvard, but law is not for me. I'm a journalist at heart." He told her about the agreement he'd made with his father. "I have a network program now, and he's accepted that this is my life. He's a great guy, and I'm extremely proud of him.

"I don't talk about my folks much, because I want to earn whatever I get, and I don't want to be associated with some of my father's high-profile cases."

"Then I won't mention him. I know your parents are proud of you. If I had a son who grew up to have your stature, values, bearing and brilliance, I'd be a very happy woman."

He swallowed heavily as he tried to get his breath back. "That is the most wonderful thing anyone has ever said to me, and I hope you meant every word." If he were lucky, maybe he could give her a chance at that happiness. Filling up with emotion, he figured he should change the tenor of things.

"I'd better feed you."

"I'll help you, otherwise I'll have to clean the kitchen."

"Where did that logic come from?"

"The person who cooks doesn't clean. Didn't you know? When my mother and I lived together after my father died, that was the rule. We got along just fine."

"Am I supposed to remember that?" he asked her.

"That's right," she said, as bold as he. "And we'll get along just fine."

Laughter poured out of him. He was happy, and he had to kiss her. Fire be damned.

"Maybe you'd better get out of here," he said, his breath coming in pants after he pulled his tongue out of her mouth.

"Not to worry. I always heard that a man can't make love on an empty stomach."

"Whoever told you that didn't know *this* man."

She raised an eyebrow. "Really? Where's the rice? It takes seventeen minutes after the water boils, but shrimp is done in five minutes."

He set the table in the kitchen, deliberately, because he didn't want her to feel like a guest, but like a woman who was where she belonged. "Unless there're at least eight people at that table, it's a very unfriendly setting, at least to me."

"I eat in my kitchen every night," she said. "I grew up eating in the kitchen. When I was little, we didn't have a dining room. But anyone would be miserable eating alone in your dining room, it's bigger than my living room."

"Were you unhappy as a child? I mean, was your family poor?"

"It didn't seem that way to me then, but after I went to college, I saw so many differences between the way I lived and the lives of a lot of other children, that I realized my family existed on a lower level. My dad was an insurance salesman, and mother had an office job at Sears. So we got on all right. They were extremely close, perpetual lovers, and my mother never got over my father's death. She stopped enjoying living. They only had one child, because my father said it would be all he could do to educate me.

"I went to dental school at NYU, because New York was the one place I knew that a person could get a job working any time of day or night that was convenient. It proved to be a wise move."

The strength of his sudden urge to protect and care for her was such that it startled him. He settled for an arm around her shoulder. "I'd better go downstairs and find us some wine."

"You have a basement?"

"I don't call it that but, yes, I store wine and food there, and among other things, you'll see a big, flat-screen TV, a pool table, dartboard and things. Want to go down with me? We can take the elevator, if you like."

"Why not. Imagine an elevator in a private house. I think it's fantastic."

"Well, if I get sick, break my leg or if I have a friend who's wheelchair bound, it'll come in handy."

She gazed up at him with a sober face. "Or you've planned well for old age, yours and your parents."

"Pretty close," he said, thinking that she should have included herself.

It wasn't really a basement, but a well-planned and finished lower level. The small room that served as a wine cellar contained what she figured to be around three hundred bottles. He said she was about right. One end of the main room had the appearance of a comfortable living room, furnished with a brown leather sofa and matching chair, coffee table, lamps, music center and flat-screen television. Nearby stood a pool table. On the opposite wall stood an eight-foot bar and six bar stools.

"What's in there?" she asked, pointing to a door.

"Refrigerator, washer, dryer and pantry." He pointed out a room in which he kept firewood and kindling. "The bathroom is over there." He pointed to a door at the bottom of the stairs.

"A person could live down here. Why did you put the music center down here rather than upstairs."

"I didn't want it near the piano. When my parents visit me, I want to hear music, and one of them wants to play the piano or vice versa. And if I ever have children, this arrangement will be doubly useful." He got two bottles of wine, took her hand and pushed the elevator button. "Are you going to have children?" he asked as they stepped into the elevator. From her reflection in the mirror, he could see that she was taken aback, but it was a question to which he needed an answer.

"As soon as I get the chance," she said.

"Same here," he said and laughed to lighten the suddenly heavy air.

"The rice and asparagus are done," she said when they got back to the kitchen. By the time you sauté the shrimp, I can have the salad ready."

"Great. The shrimp will take five minutes, I'll chill the wine, and we can eat."

"I'm cleaning the kitchen," he said after they finished eating. It'll take me ten minutes. You put some wood on the fire and then have a seat. Okay?"

"I hadn't realized that you were this bossy."

"Neither had I," he said. "I always thought of it as being self-assured."

She cocked her head to the side and looked directly at him. "Bossy means telling others what to do and how to do it and expecting them to comply."

"And you don't like that?"

"It's fine if it's not directed at me."

"Suppose I say, 'Please go into the living room and have a seat, and I'll be there in about ten minutes with some wine and petit fours.' Would that sound better?"

"You're meddling with me."

He put the dishes and utensils into the dishwasher, turned on the garbage disposal unit, cleaned the countertops and reached for the light. She hadn't moved. "I guess I was teasing. If you've forgiven me, can I have a little kiss?"

She whirled around. "Who is this guy? What happened to Craig Jackson? He doesn't have a... Wait a minute." She walked over to him, put her arms around him and raised her lips for a kiss. "Did you really need a kiss?"

"Badly. I'm behaving like a saint. I haven't had any previous experience with this type of self-control, but I've had plenty at telling people what to do. So being bossy is easier."

"You laid down the rules."

"Yes, I did, and they are paying off. I'm not sorry, but from time to time, humor me."

"I have a feeling you may be serious."

"I am. It's a little easier if you aren't so close. I don't mean that. I mean...I don't know what I mean."

A bright smile lit her face. "Let's look at it this way. Married people don't spend all their time in bed."

He let out a tension-releasing laugh. Then he laughed and laughed. When he finally could get control, he said, "When they first get married, they do. Oh, trust me, they do." He turned out the light and went to the living room, where they finished the second bottle of wine, ate the petit fours and fell asleep in each other's arms.

He awakened with a start. Where was he and why was he all tied up? He saw that the fire was down to a few hot coals, and when Kisha snuggled closer to him, he knew that she, too, felt the chill. He looked at his watch, noted that they'd slept for more than three hours and decided to awaken her.

"I'm sorry to wake you up, sweetheart, but it's half past midnight. Let's turn in and get up early in the morning."

"I fell asleep? I'm sorry."

"Not to worry, sweetheart. Both of us slept. You're a warm little bundle."

"I am a *happy* little bundle. That's for sure. I don't know when I've had such a delightful sleep. Give some thought to changing your rules." She leaned to him, kissed him quickly and stood.

He watched her perfect body glide away from him and head for the stairs. "If I don't get a starry crown in afterlife, there is no justice," he said.

# Chapter 11

Kisha didn't expect Craig to knock on her door, but a girl had to be prepared for all contingencies. She took a rose-colored teddy out of the drawer with the intention of sleeping in it, but abruptly, she sat down on the side of the bed and blew out a long breath. Craig Jackson was a wealthy man with wealthy parents, a lawyer as well as a journalist, and a Harvard law-school grad. She made a mental note to ask him where he got his undergraduate degree. And he had a famous trial lawyer for a father.

After she visited his apartment in Baltimore, she assumed that its elegance reflected the level of his salary. However, the house that he used on weekends was not ordinary, but built to his specifications, and it reflected a substantial wealth.

She thought of all that he revealed about himself and his parents, wondering what, if anything, in that information explained his reluctance to talk about himself. She suspected the answer lay with his father and his law practice. Or maybe not. She wanted to meet his parents, but would she like them? And how would they react to her? She lifted her shoulder in a slight shrug. It wasn't something over which she planned to lose any sleep.

After a shower and a few minutes of pampering herself, she put on the teddy and got into bed. *If I told Noreen about these sleeping arrangements, she'd either laugh or she'd tell me I'm lying,* she thought as she drifted off in sleep.

She dressed in heavy-weight woolen pants and a cashmere sweater the next morning, put on the walking shoes she bought for the occasion and went down to the kitchen to help prepare breakfast.

"Hi," he said when she entered the kitchen. "I hope you slept well." Still holding a spatula and a pot holder, he leaned over and kissed her mouth.

"Thanks," she said, a little taken aback by the matter-of-fact kiss. She preferred not to tell him how long she'd lain awake thinking of the absurdity of the situation, wanting to put an end to it. But knowing how much he wanted more for them than they had, she had controlled the urge to get up, open the door to his room and share his bed.

"Thanks. That is a very comfortable bed."

He glanced at her, and she knew he questioned her response, but he didn't pursue the topic. "Breakfast is ready. I thought we'd go down to the river and get some fresh fish for lunch. What do you think?"

"I'm in your capable hands. I go where you go and do what you do, except when it comes to worms. I'll only fish if you bait the hooks."

He sat down at the table, reached for her hands and said

the grace. "Do you really think I'd expect you to bait your hook with a worm?"

"I'm so scared of anything that crawls that, when it comes to them, I probably don't think straight. This waffle is delicious."

"Thanks. I'll let Aunt Jemima know you enjoyed them. I have no idea how to make waffles. Want some more?"

She did, but thought it best to save what space she had left for the fresh fish they'd have for lunch. "Thanks, but I'd better be prudent. What time did you get up?"

"A little after six. I want this to be a long day." He put the dishes and pans in the dishwasher and the refuse in the garbage disposer, wiped the marble-top counter and reached for her hand. "Dress warmly. I'll meet you at the front door in fifteen minutes."

She put on her jacket and hat, wrapped a woolen scarf around her neck, got her gloves and raced back down the stairs. With the fishing gear stored in the trunk of his Mercedes, he drove them a couple of miles from his house, turned into a little road and followed it into the woods. "The river's right down there," he told her. They walked along a single-file path, and the sound of dried leaves crackling beneath their feet unnerved her. She heard what sounded like a stick crack and whirled around.

"What was that? Are there wild animals in these woods?" she asked.

He walked beside her, slung his left arm around her shoulder and said, "There's nothing to fear. We're in the woods, sweetheart, and we'll hear all kinds of sounds."

She glanced back as a black bear disappeared into the thicket. "That was a bear, but he went the other way," she said in a trembling voice.

"If he went the other way, that's good to know," he said, as if bears were of no consequence.

"Aren't you afraid of them?"

"Sure, but if I don't bother him, he won't bother me. Here we are, I'll build a fire, and you can forget about bears." He lit some kindling, put some sticks and pieces of wood on it, and sat on a nearby bench. "Bears know better than to go near a fire. You hold this while I bait the books."

She watched him put the worm on her hook. "Ugh. Someone fishes here often," she said when they found two stumps near the river's edge.

"Maybe. I put the bench there and built that fire pit. Others use it, but it's always clean." He closed his right hand over hers and threw out her line. "When you feel a tug and that red-and-white ball disappears underwater, you have a bite. Reel it in slowly and carefully."

"Okay. Do they ever fall off."

"Frequently, but a fish isn't clever, and you can catch him again minutes later with the same bait."

"Is that true, or is it male logic?"

"It's true for fish, but whether it works with women, depends upon the woman…or the man, for that matter. The best strategy in relationships is honesty." She didn't want to ask him, but he had maneuvered the conversation to a discussion of personal things, and perhaps he was looking for an opportunity to talk seriously.

"Absolutely," she said more vehemently than she'd intended. "A man shouldn't lie to a woman, neither by word nor deed, and I should know."

"Did you love him?"

"No, but I liked him a lot, enough that it hurt. He had

the bearing and the manners of a gentleman, but he didn't tell me he had a woman he'd deserted, a child that he didn't support and that at least one other woman was crawling on her knees begging him to come back to her. My friend, the dentist with whom I substitute at vacation time, saw me with the man and called him out in my presence. Then he told me in front of the man that the guy was all husks and no corn and that I shouldn't waste time with him.

"So with his help, I investigated and learned the rest. My lover had lied when he told me he was unattached, single, didn't have any children and had never lived with a woman. I hadn't asked him all that. He volunteered it."

"He sounds like a player. You're fortunate to have escaped him."

"Don't I know it! After that, I stayed away from men. Period. You sneaked up on me."

"That kind of deception and treachery hurts. I've been there," he said.

The ball on her line bobbled and sank out of sight, but she ignored it. This was more important, and if interrupted, the moment might not return. She reached out and placed a hand on his arm. "Were you in love with her?"

He sucked in his breath. "I was engaged to her, and she was wearing my ring."

"Oh, my goodness. Do you feel like telling me about it?"

"For a long time, I hid from it, wouldn't let myself think about it, and it continued to hurt. I mean it pained me. I hadn't ever opened myself to a woman before. I thought I had the world by the horns. My career was moving like a rocket, my dad had just won a case before the Supreme Court and I had a coveted six-month assignment to cover a story in Paris. She and I wrote regularly, called each other often, and when I got back to Baltimore, I went directly from the airport to her apartment.

"I'd had a key to her place ever since we became engaged, but I'd never used it. This time I did and walked in on her thrashing in bed with her lover. It's the mercy of God that I was in such shock I didn't commit a crime. I wheeled around and went home, but I was so unsettled and distraught that I couldn't get my key in the lock, and I had to get the superintendent to open the door. She called me a hundred times that evening and night, and I think she knocked on my door around eleven that night, but I didn't answer a phone or the door. Sometime the next morning, I sent her an e-mail telling her to send the ring to me by registered mail within one week, or I would sue her."

"Did she send it?"

"No. She brought it to my office. I hated to look at her, hated to see the woman I had loved grovel for forgiveness as if she didn't have a shred of dignity. Less than a month ago, she called me asking for another chance. She explained for the nth time that she betrayed my trust because she was lonely. She swore it was the only time she did that. I had taught her to need sex…on and on. It fell on deaf ears. I closed that book three years ago, and it will remain closed. For me, she does not exist.

"You claim that I don't share myself with you, and I know you're right. I've felt the difference in intimacy with you from the time we talked last night. I've told myself that if I don't make the effort, I'll lose you, and I can't stand the thought of that. It isn't easy, Kisha, but I intend to try and share everything with you, because I know it's important to you. What I'm learning is how important it is to me that you understand me and know me thoroughly."

"And I want you to know me, too, Craig. I'm open with people close to me, but since my mother passed, I've been alone, and I may be out of the habit of sharing, but it's natural for me to do so."

"What about your friend, Noreen? Don't you discuss personal things with her?"

"Not everything. I… Good grief, something's pulling hard on this line."

"Great. Maybe we *will* have fish for lunch." He covered her right hand with his own to show her how to reel in the fish, then paid attention to his own line, which seemed to have a catch. She reeled in a striped bass big enough to feed both of them, and after struggling with the line, he brought in one approximately the same size.

"I don't believe it," she said. "I actually caught a fish. Let's go home and cook it."

He seemed to have been struck by something, for he stared at her with a facial expression that could only be described as vulnerable. She walked over to him and slid the back of her right hand over his cheek. "What is it, hon? Did I do something?"

He shook his head as if clearing it. "No. I don't think so. Do you really like it here? I mean do you like my home?"

"I love it. It's so much like you, like the way I see you. It's a wonderful house."

He put the fish in a metal box, handed her the rods, picked up the container of bait and tools and said to her, "When you said, 'Let's go home,' I was reminded that last night was the first time that building truly felt like home to me. Come on. We'll put these in the trunk. Then let's walk along the riverbank for a while."

"Won't the bears smell the fish?"

"Good point. Let's drive to the park. Bears don't go there. We can get some coffee and walk a bit. It's nice there in winter."

"What a relief," she said when he drove off. "Mr. Bear can trash somebody else's car in his search for fresh fish, or he can catch his own."

He parked at the entrance to the Marriottsville state park, bought coffee from a vendor, and they sat in the car and drank it.

"Craig, are you satisfied that we can surmount the obstacles facing us? I came here this weekend hoping that we'd be closer to each other as a result of this sojourn."

"A lot has happened to me this weekend, Kisha, and it's all for the good. I've rid myself of some old cobwebs in my life, stuff that I didn't realize interfered with our relationship.

"I understand now what my dad was telling me when he said that, before they married, Mom told him that she needed more of him, that she needed him to share himself, his dreams, goals, successes, failures, loves and hates, that she didn't know him. What I feel inside is stronger and deeper. How do you feel about things?"

"It's the same with me. You found a place in my heart the day we met, yet something was lacking, and I told you about that. But since we've been together here, my feelings have changed. I can't explain it, but I have a warm, happy feeling of contentment."

Having a part of someone else in your life isn't so bad, Craig said to himself as he stood on the back deck of his house scaling fish. Spending the weekend with Kisha, seeing her at seven o'clock in the morning with her hair down and without lipstick or makeup was not the same as spending time with her in restaurants and other public paces. He could get used to being with her, and as he thought of it, wasn't that what he wanted? *You need a dog,* an inner voice said. "No I don't," he said aloud. "I need kids."

Stunned at hearing his own voice, he whirled around and released a long and heavy breath. She hadn't come back downstairs yet, and for that, he was grateful. The sound of her coming down the stairs sent his heart into a wild race. He leaned against the kitchen counter, steadied himself and acknowledged that he had to make a decision. A half smile played around his lips. He made a pot of coffee, and looked out of the window thinking how much he would enjoy being snowbound there with Kisha.

"What are we having with the fish, and what can I do to move this baby along?" She walked up behind him and wrapped her arms around his waist. Didn't she know what feeling her hard nipples against his back did to him? Suspecting that she did, he turned around within the circle of her arms and held her to him.

"You can bake those two Idaho potatoes in the microwave, peel them, and cut them into strips lengthwise." He turned on the oven. "While the fish and potatoes are baking, I'll make a salad."

"Works for me." She scrubbed the two potatoes and put them in the microwave. Ten minutes later, she said. "What next?"

He sprayed cooking oil on a sheet of aluminum foil, placed the potato strips on it, squeezed lemon juice over them, sprinkled pepper, sprayed them again and put them in the oven. He did the same with the filleted fish, wrapped it securely in foil and put it in the oven. "I've washed the lettuce, so the salad will be ready in a minute."

After lunch, he poured two cups of fresh coffee. "Let's drink this in the living room in front of the fire. That fireplace is one of the things I love most about this house."

"I love it, too. Are you going to play for me? Even if this piano is out of tune, I want to hear you play."

"Of course I will. What would you like me to play?"

"Whatever pleases you. Something that you particularly enjoy playing."

He would rather play in the evening with the fire in the fireplace as their only light, *because she definitely was not going up those steps alone tonight.* He had nearly gone out of his mind the night before, knowing that she was lying less than ten feet from him and that if he had gone to her, she would not have denied him. But though he had wanted her almost to the point of desperation, he was playing for higher stakes, and he meant to win.

He lowered the blinds at the nearest window and closed them, flicked on the wall sconce near the piano and sat down. She picked up a chair at the dining table, brought it over to the piano and sat down beside him.

As he usually did when he began to play, Craig flexed his fingers and sat forward on the bench. Then, his long, lean fingers hit the first notes of a prelude by Chopin and, after casting a quick glance to see if she liked it, he settled down to enjoying one of the reasons why he'd learned to play the piano.

"That was wonderful," she said when it ended. "You could have had a career as a pianist."

"I don't think so. I love music, and I love to play, but it isn't a singular passion for me. I'd rather be a reporter."

"But you're accomplished. I know practically every note in that prelude, and you gave every one of them your loving attention."

He couldn't help laughing. "You're a true poet. I never thought that way about playing a piece I enjoyed. Giving it my loving attention, eh? Not bad. He rubbed his hands together as if washing them. Looked toward the ceiling and launched into "Take Five," a jazz composition by Paul Desmond, that had Kisha snapping her fingers.

"That thing's written in five-sevenths time, Craig. How could you read it?"

Hmm. There was something she had yet to tell him. "I didn't read it. I learned it from ear first. Then I read it. How much music did you study, and which instrument do you play?"

"I studied piano for about five years, but my father died, and my mother had to save what money there was for my college education. I haven't touched a piano since I came to Maryland."

He got up. "Play something, something that you can sing. I've always wondered about your voice. It's so musical and soothing."

"All right, but don't judge me harshly if I make mistakes. I'm not in your league." He sat in his favorite chair, facing the fire and closed his eyes. Anyone with a speaking voice like hers could sing.

After playing a few scales, practice notes, she played the introduction to "Willow, Weep for Me," and he sat up straight. Her rich mezzo soprano filled the room, and although she played it well, it was not her playing that interested him, but her singing.

"I'm surprised that you aren't a professional singer. You

have a beautiful voice. Do you know a lullaby? I'd love to hear you sing one."

"I'll sing the Brahms if you'll play it."

At the end of it, he walked over to her and hugged her. "We make beautiful music together."

"Yeah," she said. "In the kitchen, in the living room and…oops!"

"Chicken. I'll say it, since you don't have the nerve. In the bedroom."

She hid her face against his chest. "You embarrass me."

"No such thing. You started it and got cold feet. Let's go upstairs to my den. I want to show you my scrapbooks." He thought better of the idea, because he didn't need to be near a bed with her, at least not yet. "Scratch that. I'll bring a couple of them down stairs."

His cell phone rang as he reached the second level. "Hello, Dad. How's Mom?"

"We're both just fine. I called you at your apartment. Where are you?"

"I'm at my place in Marriottsville."

"In this weather? How's it there?"

"Cold and dreary. I brought Kisha with me. We needed to get to know each other, and so far it's going great."

"I hope you're learning that the more you give, the more you get."

"And the easier it is to give. I'm making progress."

"Glad to hear it. She must be quite a woman."

"She is. I'd…I'd like to bring her with me when I come out to see you and Mom at Christmas."

"I was just about to suggest that. Are you thinking of making it permanent?"

"She suits me, Dad. When I add up what we have in common, it's eerie. You'll see."

"What does she do besides practice dentistry?"

"She's a very good painter and recently had a successful show. She plays the piano well and has a beautiful voice. She also has a strong humanitarian streak."

"Well, if the chemistry's there, and if she's willing to give me some grandchildren, it sounds ideal."

"I hope you're not planning to ask her that question."

"No, but I'm not above dropping a hint. Give her my love, and tell her I hope to meet her soon."

"Thanks, Dad. Tell Mom I love her as always."

He hung up and walked on to his den, though not with the quick steps that took him up the stairs. He'd just committed himself to Kisha. It had simmered in his thoughts for weeks. Recently, he knew it in his heart, felt it in every molecule of his body and now, he had all but admitted it to his father. But was he ready to make it official? Once he did that, there was no turning back. He was a man who dotted every *i* and crossed every *t,* and he had to be sure. He selected scrapbooks from his high school and college days and went back to her.

"It gets dark earlier and earlier this time of year," she said, almost sadly. "I love the long days of summer."

He sat on the floor before the fire, spread the scrapbooks around him, and she joined him. "What bothers me, is that, for the next couple of months, the darkness seems to last longer and longer," he said.

She opened one of the scrap books and pointed to the picture of a boy smiling cockily. "Who's this?"

"I was thirteen."

"Hmm. You've changed so much."

She was right, but that was a different time, and now he

was about a man's business. Moreover, he no longer believed that he could have whatever he wanted, no matter how hard he worked for it. He wanted Kisha, and he believed that she loved him, but he knew that she was as good at self-denial as he. He opened his college scrapbook. Better to keep her thinking about him as a man, not as a child.

*He promised to be open, let me know and understand him, and he's keeping his word,* she thought as she looked at his trophies for debating, reporting, football, and his diploma. "So you graduated magna cum laude?" she asked. "Why am I not surprised? How did you miss being summa cum laude?"

The question seemed to bring back pleasant memories to him. "I got a C in ancient history, because there were no records of some of the events we studied, and a lot of that stuff didn't seem plausible to me, so I argued against it. The professor didn't find that amusing. It didn't much matter. I wasn't studying for grades. I wanted to learn everything that I could."

As they went through the scrapbooks, his life unfolded like a beautifully choreographed ballet. He had always kept to himself. She saw no pictures of him constantly with the same buddies, only with the members of his fraternity. In one of the photos, she recognized the man who'd catered the reception for her art show.

"Were you and Jerry buddies in school?"

"Not really, but we lived on the same floor in the dorm, and we were friends. I didn't have a buddy, a guy that I hung around with. I didn't find anyone enough like me to put up with my way of life."

"What do you mean by that?"

"I didn't go to every dance, every party and date every good-looking girl on campus. My folks crammed it into my head that if I bombed in college, I wouldn't get another chance, so I tried to learn everything that I could. I suppose I was considered boring."

She cocked an eyebrow and looked straight at him. "You're kidding, I hope."

"No. I'm dead serious. I fitted in at Harvard, because that place was full of eggheads." He looked at his watch. "I'd better check on the dinner."

"I enjoyed this journey through your youth. Thanks for sharing it with me. I wish I had scrapbooks like these of my life. How may I help with dinner?"

"You can't. Everything's done except the filet mignon. I only have to warm stuff. After I get it in order, I want to stretch out for a few minutes and change. We can eat about seven-thirty, so if you want to take a nap or whatever…" He didn't bother to finish the sentence.

"I want to put on a dress," she said. "I'm not going to eat filet mignon looking frumpy."

She loved his deep rolling laughter. "You wouldn't look frumpy if you'd been out logging."

And so, without articulating it, they agreed to dress for dinner. "I'll be down a little after seven," she said. That would give her time for a good soak in a tub filled with bubbles. She could hardly wait.

He liked her in red, and she wanted him to have his fill of it. Besides, she thought, as she dressed with an eye to the postdinner part of the evening, red was sexy. *If he intends to prolong this celibacy act, I've got news for him. It isn't going to happen.*

The dress sleeves stopped midway between her elbow

and wrist, but that was the only concession to modesty. The
split in the front of the long, silk-jersey sheath stopped
twelve inches above her knee. She shrugged her shoulders
at the exposed cleavage, and walked around the room,
testing her spike-heel shoes. With her hair below her shoulders, long diamond chip earrings dangling from her ears
and her favorite perfume completing her attire, she kissed
caution goodbye and headed down the stairs at seven-thirty.

She nearly slipped when she saw him gazing up at her
from the foot of the stairs. And as if her perilous slip was
the cue he wanted, he dashed up the stairs to meet her. "I've
seen you as all kinds of women—a dentist, a serious professional in a TV interview, a painter dressed as a gypsy,
and fisherwoman in below-freezing temperatures. You are
always perfect and always beautiful. But I never dreamed
you were a siren."

"I'm not."

"Don't tell me, sweetheart, I'm looking at you. Dinner's
ready, so I think we'd better eat. I'm getting warm in this
jacket." He put an arm around her as they walked down the
stairs and on to the dining room. "I don't serve filet mignon
and lobster in the kitchen," he said, when she raised an
eyebrow. After seating her, he brought their first course, slices
of cold lobster in lobster sauce garnished with watercress.

"This is one of the best meals I've eaten in a long time,"
she said near the end of the meal, as she savored the cheese,
a blue-veined, English Stilton. "I'm not sure I have space
left for dessert."

"It's simple. Chocolate sauce over poached pears and
espresso coffee. We can have it in the living room."

She was not about to disagree with him, no matter what
he said. So far, he'd charted the weekend, and his vision

for it had been filled with fruitful results. But the evening was also going according to Kisha's plan, and she had a feeling that he knew it. She sashayed into the living room, giving him a good look at her back action, and sat on the sofa. When he entered the room ten minutes later, bringing their dessert and espresso, she patted the seat beside her and half raised an eyebrow.

"Sit here," she said. "After all that wine, I may want to put my head on your shoulder."

"You only drank two glasses, and considering what you ate, that's not much wine. But if you want to put your head on my shoulder, I couldn't be more pleased."

"I like this," she said of the dessert. "It's delicious and very light. You're almost the perfect man." She drained her coffee cup. "I mean if I'd made you myself, I couldn't have produced a better specimen." That said, she leaned her head against his shoulder, put her right arm across his body and snuggled close to him.

"Would you like some music?"

"Uh-huh, but I don't want you to move away from me." She reached up and kissed his cheek.

"You said those nice thing about my cooking, and—"

"The food was great, Craig, and this entire weekend is etched in my brain as a beautiful interlude that I'll never forget." She felt him stiffen as if anticipating something unpleasant. "But," she continued, "I was talking about you. And if I think you are wonderful, that's my right." She eased her hand inside his jacket and stroked his chest. "Isn't that so?"

"Yeah," he growled, as her fingers teased his right areola. "What are you up to?"

"Me? Nothing."

He traced his fingers from inside of her arm at the elbow down to her waist. "Are you sure you don't want me to put on a CD?" She shook her head. Maybe he'd get the message after a while. "I'm fine here with you. Honest."

"I want to dance with you."

Now that was something that she could support. The man was playing her game. "Something nice and soft. How about Luther Vandross's 'Here and Now.' Do you have that?"

"I do, but how about 'Always and Forever?' That's my favorite. I may have both on this collection. The guy had a great voice. Too bad he's gone." She released him, and immediately she was bereft of his nearness, but not as she had been in the past. She didn't have the feeling of having been dropped from a heavenly perch to the pit of a ravine.

When she heard the first strains of "Here and Now," she looked up at him, and he held out both hands to her. She floated into his arms and let the man and the music carry her away. The song ended, and as "Always and Forever" began, he whispered in her ear, "That's what I want with you."

She missed a step, recovered and let him feel her whole body in his arms as he danced to the rhythm while barely moving his feet. She didn't answer him, because she didn't believe in taking anything for granted.

His right hand dropped to her buttocks, and she responded automatically and without thought, by widening her stance, a natural invitation that he didn't miss. "Kiss me," she whispered. "I've waited all day for it and for you."

She could feel his erection against her belly, and she gripped him tighter as his tongue slid into her mouth. She sucked him deeper into her as heat like live sparks showered throughout her body, singeing her nerve endings and building a fire for him in the pit of her. Both of his hands cupped her buttocks and held her tightly against him letting her feel his need until her moans filled the air.

"Tell me what you want. I'll do anything for you. Anything."

She was beyond words. He hadn't been inside of her in weeks, and now that she knew she'd have him, she thought she'd go insane. She grabbed his hand and put it on her breasts. He released her left breast, and swallowed her nipple into his mouth.

"Oh, my," she screamed, holding his head and undulating wildly against his body. As if he'd been starved for months, he suckled her until she felt the liquid running down her leg.

"Please," she whispered, panting for breath. "Take me to bed. I want you inside of me." He picked her up and carried her up the stairs to his room.

He asked if he could undress her and she nodded her head. The dressed pooled at her feet, and he lifted her, put her on the bed and stared down at her. Then he knelt and removed her shoes, leaned over and removed her bra. She cupped her left breast, and he pulled its nipple into his mouth and devoured it ravenously. She tried to remove her bikini panties, but he stopped her.

"Don't deprive me of that privilege." He undressed, never taking his eyes from hers. He kicked off his shoes, removed his socks and stepped closer to the bed. She reached out to touch him, and he was fully engorged. Excited, she licked her lips, leaned down and surrounded him with her mouth.

"Don't do that, baby," he said, pulling away from her. "I could explode any minute, and that's not what we need. He hooked his thumbs in the straps of her bikini panties and pulled them off her, then he leaned over and traced his prize with the tip of his tongue. She shifted her hips from side to side, spread her legs and held up her arms to him in a gesture as old as Eve.

He covered her with his body, and his lips traced her ears, forehead and eyes. His tongue dipped into the hollow of her throat, and then his lips grazed the spot in short sucking motions.

"Kiss me," she whispered.

"I *am* kissing you. There's no hurry. I'm waking up tomorrow morning with you in my arms." His lips covered hers, and she opened, took him in and pulling deeply to let him know how much she wanted him. He sampled every crevice, every centimeter of her mouth, pulling out and shoving back in to remind her of what he planned to do to her.

"Please, honey. I'm hot as fire."

His tongue traced the route to her navel, lingered there, and when her body began to weave and dance, he hooked her unruly knees over his shoulders and thrust his tongue into her, sucking, licking and kissing until she felt the heat at the bottom of her feet.

"Please, honey, I'm going to come and I want you inside of me."

"Don't worry, I will be. Tell me you love me."

"I do. I do. I always did. Craig!"

He kissed his way up her body, wrapped her in his arms and smiled down at her, sending her heart into a tailspin. "Take me in baby."

She bent her knees, reached down, led him to her and held her breath until that moment when at last she could feel him.

"Oh, yes," he said as he sank into her and began to move.

Within a minute, she could feel vibrations rip through her body. He thrust rhythmically, all the while looking into her eyes. He increased the pace, and she could feel the pumping and swelling as she seemed to get fuller and fuller. If she didn't explode she'd die.

"Honey, I can't stand this. I…I think I'm dying."

"No you're not. You're loving me."

"But…" The quivering of her thighs must have been a signal to him because he thrust with such power that she could hardly keep up with him.

"Be still, baby, and I'll give you what you need." He moved with speed and power until she screamed, "You're drowning me. I want to burst, I… Oh, Craig. I love you. I love you." She collapsed, so shaken that she didn't hear his confession of love for her when he seemed to come apart in her arms.

Hours later, after they slept, made love, slept and made love again, she awakened when he sat on the edge of the bed, handed her a mug of warm milk and half a dozen gingersnaps.

"Thanks, hon. I'm not sure I have enough energy to eat."

"You're welcome. I'll always take care of you." When she finished, he put the empty cup on his night table. "I love you, Kisha, and nothing is ever going to change that." He got into bed, put his arms around her, and her head on his shoulder. "Let's go to sleep. If you want or need anything during the night, don't hesitate to wake me."

# Chapter 12

Kisha awakened to sunlight streaming in her face and was about to turn over and go back to sleep when, abruptly, she sat up. What time was it and what day was it? Should she have been at work? She rubbed her eyes and looked around. What? Where was she? It came back to her then. The hours of loving, of losing herself in him, of his loving kisses and the way that he'd cherished her. She'd lost perception as to where she ended and he began. She hadn't dreamed that human beings could feel and experience what she found with Craig that night. She rolled over, brought his pillow to her breasts, hugged and kissed it, sniffing the musky scent of his body and of their lovemaking. Overwhelmed by her feelings, she threw her arms wide and embraced the world. Where was he? She looked toward the night table. Ten o'clock. She'd never slept that late.

She slid out of the covers and went to her bathroom,

showered and then dressed. She couldn't wait to get to him, to hold him and know again that feeling of oneness. She ran down the stairs and into the kitchen, but he wasn't there. Fear began a slow curl up her spine, and she walked slowly and tentatively to the living room, where he knelt before the fireplace, brushing away ashes from the hearth.

"Hi," she managed to say.

He turned sharply, jumped up and looked at her. "Hi. I wanted to bring you breakfast in bed, but I didn't want to wake you up. I knew you were tired, because you went to sleep so late. How do you feel…about us, I mean?" The words tumbled out of him.

He stood there, open and vulnerable. Words wouldn't come. How could she explain to him all that seethed inside of her? Desperate, her feet moved, and then she opened wide her arms and sped to him.

"I love you. Oh, Craig, I love you so much."

He picked her up, hugged her, spun her around and laughed. "Do you…is it all right? Did you have that same empty feeling when you didn't find me beside you?"

"I hadn't even thought about that. No. I didn't. After I figured out where I was and why, I felt as if the whole world was mine."

"Thank goodness. For me, what we had last night was nothing less than sweet communion. If you had told me it made no difference, I'd have been devastated. I set the table. It's too late for breakfast. Brunch consists of drumsticks, popovers, scrambled eggs, mixed fresh fruit and coffee. I only have to warm the popovers and chicken and scramble the eggs. Personally, I feel like adding champagne to that, but I don't drink if I plan to drive within three hours."

They prepared the food, sat down at the kitchen table, said

grace and began to eat. "Will you spend Christmas with me
at my parents' home? I want you to come with me, and my
dad asked me to bring you. He also sent regards to you."

"Uh…what will your mother say?"

"She'll be happy. The two of you have a great deal in
common."

"That's right. She's a pediatrician. What's your father's
name?" If he was reluctant to tell her or if he did so grudg-
ingly, she would know that nothing had changed.

"John Fentriss Jackson. He wanted to give me that
name, but Mom objected. She said I should have my own,
and she named me Craig Hayden Jackson. Hayden is her
maiden name. I like it a lot better than I like Dad's name.
At any rate, I'm glad she won that battle, because he's
famous, and I don't have to battle with a constant comparison to him."

She relaxed. It was all right. "On the other hand, Craig,
he doesn't have to live up to the standard you've set, either."

For a minute, he seemed shocked. Then laughter rolled
out of him, a sound that she could never get enough of.
"Attagirl. Every guy needs a fan. If it's all right with you,
I'd like to leave around three. You ought to be home before
dark to check things out."

"Fortunately, Bingo is my only pet, and he doesn't have
to be fed."

A quizzical expression settled on his face. "Bingo? Oh,
you mean that little lamb."

"Right. I'll be ready to go in half an hour." She dashed
up the stairs, found the linen closet and changed the
bedding on her bed, packed and knocked on his bedroom
door. He didn't answer, so she took her bag down the stairs.
He met her at the foot of the staircase.

"I don't like the looks of this weather, so I suggest we leave right now." He got her coat and scarf, helped her into the coat and wrapped the scarf around her neck. He looked down at her for such a long time that she began to fidget.

"I simply can't get used to what's happened to me this weekend," he said in a voice tinged with awe. "I've loved you for a long time, but it's different now." He trapped her between himself and the wall beside the front door. "You take my breath away. I'm enchanted with you."

She let her right hand stroke the side of his face. "It happened to me, too, and I'm so happy. I didn't dream that I could be so happy."

His lips brushed hers and she opened to him. His tongue slipped into her mouth and, for a second, dueled with hers. Then, he withdrew. "Baby, I have to drive. Our day will come."

"When do you want to leave for Seattle?"

"Christmas Eve morning. Can you get someone to fill in for you, say for a week?"

"I'll ask Gerald Harper, and I'll phone the parents of the children who come on Thursday afternoon to contact Gerald if they have an emergency."

"Good. Then it's settled."

"Girl, you got to tell me about the weekend. You know you didn't go off by yourself. If you weren't with Craig Jackson, I wanna know where you got that glow on your face. I sure wish I could have a weekend that would make me look like that. You happy?"

She laughed. "Fortunately, I don't have to answer all of your questions. Yes, I'm happy. Oh, Noreen. I'm about to fly out of my skin."

"Lord, help me. I'm gon' lose the best neighbor I ever had."

"Nobody's asked me to go anywhere or do anything."

"No? But the writing is on the wall, honey. That man loves you. I knew it all the time, and now, you know it, too. Well, let me know when."

In the ensuing week, Kisha bought gifts for Noreen, her receptionist, her godchild, Craig and his parents, wrapped them and put the packages in a suitcase separate from her own things. She was on a natural high, and she prayed she would stay that way.

Craig called Kisha when he awakened each morning, before he went to bed each night and brought lunch to her at her office each noon.

"You're spoiling me, Craig," she told him when he brought her lunch on her last day at work. "Suppose I get used to this?"

"It's what I'm counting on. I want you to feel that you can't live without me."

"I already can't," she murmured.

His arms eased around her. "I'm practicing restraint, because I'll have to behave around my mother."

She kissed his chin. "You'd better. They won't like me if they see you taking too many liberties with me."

A grin spread across his face. "It's all right with you if I take the liberties, but don't let Mom or Dad catch me at it. Right?"

"More or less."

He brushed her lips with a quick kiss. "I'll be there at seven tomorrow morning." On the way out, he stopped at Regine's desk, and gave her a small package wrapped with a big purple velvet bow.

"Thanks, Mr. Jackson. If you didn't belong to Dr. Moran, I'd hug you. Have a great Christmas."

"Thanks. I consider myself hugged."

The next morning, they got through security without becoming exasperated and boarded the plane at nine o'clock, ten minutes to flight time. He stored their carry-on luggage and offered her her choice of window or aisle seats.

"Your legs are long. I'll take the window. Why did you splurge on first class?"

"It's a six-hour flight. Do you think I'd give you less than I can afford?"

The steward served breakfast, but she declined coffee, explaining that she intended to sleep. "Would you please give us a couple of blankets," he asked a passing steward. As soon as she finished eating, he wrapped the blankets around her, put a pillow beneath her head and reclined her seat.

"I love you a lot," she murmured a few minutes later.

Their plane landed in Seattle at twelve noon, and at one-fifteen, he rang the doorbell of his parents' home.

"Don't you have a key?"

"Yes, but they will want the privilege of opening their door to you." He held his breath. They had to love her, because he was never going to let her go.

The door opened and a tall, attractive woman stepped forward with arms wide-open and enveloped Kisha in a warm and loving embrace. "I'm Avery Jackson. Welcome. I'm so happy that you agreed to spend the holiday with us." She held out a hand. "You know without being told that this man is Craig's father, John."

Avery looked at Craig then, her face wreathed in smiles. "Welcome home, son. You were always a winner."

Marbles seemed to rattle in Kisha's belly as John Fentriss Jackson studied her. Suddenly, his eyes sparkled and his face lit up like sunshine as she'd seen Craig's do so many times.

"Welcome to my home and, I hope, to my family," he said and embraced her in a quick hug. "My boy always had good taste." He looked at Craig, nodded and winked.

If there was a test, she supposed she'd just passed it. "I'll show you to your room," Avery said, "unless you want to share with Craig. These modern young people don't wait for marriage."

"My own room suits me. Thank you," she managed to say, taken aback as she was by the woman's suggestion.

"I suppose Craig brought you first class, and that you're not hungry, so rest if you like, and we'll have tea or coffee and snacks about three. John eats dinner late, between seven-thirty and eight. Is that all right with you? If not, I'll feed you earlier." She paused and appeared thoughtful. "I see that Craig feels deeply for you. It's written all over him, and he's so proud of you. You can't imagine how happy I am."

"Thank you. I…I got a warm feeling the moment I met you."

"Same here. We'll talk after you get settled. Craig's room is diagonally across the hall to the left. Come down whenever you're ready."

Kisha looked around. It wasn't ostentatious, but the Jackson's wealth was evident. What she saw from the time she walked through the door was taste, and she could see that Craig's background had informed his outlook and his behavior.

She showered and slipped into a brick-red, woolen crepe sheath that had long sleeves and showed no cleavage. She combed down her hair and added gold hoop earrings, shoes with two-inch heels and subtle perfume.

The family had gathered in the living room before a roaring fire in the huge marble-front fireplace beside which stood the tallest indoor Christmas tree that she'd ever seen. The scent of bayberry, pine, mulled wine and spices teased her senses, and she had a moment of sadness. Craig saw her steps falter, went to meet her and took her fully into his arms.

"What's the matter? Are you all right."

"Yes. When I smelled that mulled wine, I remembered the last Christmas my mother was with me. She always had it for the holidays. She made Christmas so festive. I haven't experienced a family Christmas since she died, and that's been eleven years. But don't worry. I'm fine."

"You look so lovely. Come sit beside me." She sat with him on the sofa, knowing that his parents watched them closely.

"I'm going in the kitchen and cut some chestnuts. Come with me, Kisha," John said. "We'll never get acquainted if Craig keeps you to himself. I hope you like them. Hot, roasted chestnuts are among our favorite things to munch on this time of year."

"I love them, but I've never cut them." She walked with him into one of the largest and most attractive kitchens she'd seen firsthand. "This is lovely and very practical. I'd love to cook in this kitchen. Hmm. And something smells delicious."

"Cookie's having a nap, but you can be sure she has the food under control." He opened a bag of chestnuts and began to cut them. "Craig is enchanted with you. He says you make him happy, and that you have a lot in common. From what he tells me, you also have a great deal in common with his mother." He stopped his chore, and she looked him in the eye when he asked her, "Do you love him? I mean, do you have any reservations about him?"

"None. I love him, more every hour. He's…he's so wonderful. He's…" She threw up her hands. "He's my life."

"I believe you. I've never seen him so happy. Looking at the two of you together makes me want to sing and shout. If you ever need my support, know that you have it."

"I thought I'd have to go in there and get you," Craig said when they returned.

"Why? You're a chip off the old block," she said with a broad smile. "Do you exchange gifts tonight or tomorrow morning, and does your mother dress for dinner tonight? Never mind. I'll ask her."

"We open gifts after dinner tonight."

She walked over to Avery. "Do you dress for dinner tonight? If you do, so will I."

Avery Jackson looked at Kisha with a wicked grin. "Wonderful. I love it. Wait until those two guys discover that they have to put on a jacket and tie."

"But Craig voluntarily did that last weekend when we had dinner at his place."

"You have no idea what a compliment that was to you. He usually has to be asked and then cajoled. I'll get us some tea, and Cookie left us a plate of goodies in the refrigerator. After tea, we can rest or do whatever we like. It'll be a long night." They separated, and Kisha brought her gifts down and placed them under the tree. Craig intercepted her as she got back to her room.

"Come here. I need to hold you." He hugged her close and kissed her nose. "I'm not getting into any heavy stuff with those two deterrents down the hall there. My mother is excited about you. I knew my dad would love you, because he's a man, and he sees what I see."

"Lord forbid. He'll want to know how many grandchildren he's getting, and your mother will want to be sure that I'll take your temperature, feed you chicken soup and look after you when you have a cold."

He stared at her. "How'd you know?"

"'Cause men are concerned with lineage and women with nurturing. Here's a kiss. I need a nap."

After a dinner of roast goose, wild rice pilaf, broiled fluted mushrooms, asparagus, green salad, assorted cheeses, sour lime pie and coffee, they played Christmas music in the living room.

"How about playing some carols, Craig?" his father said.

"I will if Kisha will sing a couple."

"'Sweet Little Jesus Boy' and 'The Christmas Song,'" she said, sang them and began what proved to be a rousing family sing-along. John announced that it was time for him to play Santa Claus, and he handed each person their gifts. Kisha had bought a black beaded evening bag for Avery, A Montblanc pen-and-pencil set for Craig with his engraved initials and two leather-bound biographies of Marcus Aurelius, one by Anthony Birley and the other by Henry Dwight Sedgwick for John.

"How did you guess I'd love this?" John asked her, his face the epitome of surprise.

"Craig told me that you love biographies and that you had just become interested in ancient history. No ancient ruler is more fascinating that Marcus Aurelius. At least not to me."

Avery hugged and kissed Kisha. "Thank you. This is precisely my taste, and I will use it happily for years to come."

Kisha received a pearl necklace from Craig, and a teardrop diamond pendant on a platinum chain from his parents.

"Breakfast at ten tomorrow," Avery said. "That'll give us a chance to sleep late." Everyone said good-night, and Craig held Kisha's hand as they headed up the stairs.

"Do you want to come in?" she asked when they reached her door.

"I'll be over in a minute. Leave the door slightly open."

The large, lustrous white pearls glistened against her shimmering green dinner gown. In her room, two hands covered her eyes, and she turned into his arms.

"Thanks for my gift and for the most perfect Christmas of my life," he said and would have covered her mouth with his if she hadn't stepped back, traced her neckline with her right index finger and smiled at him.

"Thanks for these beautiful pearls. I've never owned anything so lovely."

A seeming happiness illuminated his face, and he covered her mouth with his and ran his tongue over the seams of her lips seeking entrance. Already starved for him and longing to experience again the loving he gave her during the last night they spent in his Marriottsville home, she pulled him into her and gripped his buttocks, telling him without words what she needed.

"Take it slowly, sweetheart. I'm half-crazy wanting you."

"I'll take whatever you've got," she said, bold, brazen and hungry for him.

"What do you want."

"You know what I want. I want you."

He unzipped her dress, let it fall to the floor, lifted her out of it and put her on her bed. She kicked off her shoes and reached for him. He stepped out of his pants, kicked off his shoes and turned to face the bed. She leaned forward, yanked down his shorts and began caressing him.

"Knowing that you want me just blows my mind," he said, crawled into bed and covered her body with his. He sucked the nipple of her left breast into his mouth. Within minutes, he had her rocking and begging for his entrance.

He slid down and tested her with his tongue, sucking, nipping, kissing and plunging. When he touched the G-spot, she flung herself up to him for more of the thrill that he sent plowing through her. "Please. I want you now."

He kissed his way back up her body and plunged into her. He rode her so fast and furiously that she thought she'd die from the thrill of it. And then, he dropped her into a pit as orgasm consumed her, and his kisses exhilarated her. Her entire body trembled when he flung her into ecstasy, groaned as if in agony and gave himself to her.

She lay beneath him, thoroughly spent. Minutes passed, he got out of bed, and she thought he went to the bathroom. But he came back with a towel draped around his waist and hips and dropped to his knees.

"Kisha, I love you as I've never loved anyone. Will you be my wife? I'll take good care of you and our children. I'll be faithful to you, and I'll love you as long as I breathe."

"Yes. Yes. I want to be your wife. Oh, Craig. I'm so happy." He slipped a two-carat diamond on the third finger of her left hand. "How soon can we get married?"

"I think I can manage it in six weeks. Are two children enough, or do you want three?"

"If you give me two, I'll be deliriously happy, but I'll take as many as you give me. Truthfully, I'd rather not raise an only child."

"Neither would I."

He crawled back into bed, took her into his arms and, with her head on his shoulder, she went to sleep.

The next morning, keyed up from his loving, she dressed and went down to the dining room for breakfast. Craig's parents sat at the table with expressions of expectancy on their faces. When Craig joined them at the table, she held out her left hand to the man and woman who would be her in-laws.

John Fentriss walked around the table and hugged her. "This is one time my prayers were answered swiftly. Congratulations, son. Your mother and I were hoping and praying that this is what we'd see this morning." He smiled at Kisha. "Welcome to our family."

"Yes," Avery said. "This is truly one of the happiest moments of my life. I'm happy for Craig. But I'm just as happy for John and me, because I know we will grow to love you dearly." Tears dampened her cheeks. "I never dreamed we would be so fortunate."

"Neither did I," Craig and Kisha said in unison. "Neither did I."

* * * * *

# REQUEST YOUR FREE BOOKS!

## 2 FREE NOVELS
## PLUS 2 FREE GIFTS!

KIMANI™
ROMANCE

### Love's ultimate destination!

KROM09

# HELP CELEBRATE
# ARABESQUE'S
## 15TH ANNIVERSARY!

**15**
**ARABESQUE®**

*19  40  44  37  6*
*30*

## 2009 marks Arabesque's
## 15th anniversary!

Help us celebrate by telling us about your
most special memories and moments with
Arabesque books. Entries will be judged by
the Arabesque Anniversary Committee
based on which are the most touching and
well written. Fifteen lucky winners will
receive as a prize a full-grain leather duffel
bag with the Arabesque anniversary logo.

VISIT **WWW.MYSPACE.COM/KIMANIPRESS**
FOR THE COMPLETE OFFICIAL RULES

KPI5ARACONTEST